THE
CLACKITY

THE
CLAC

KITY

A Blight Harbor Novel

LORA SENF

Illustrated by
ALFREDO CÁCERES

ATHENEUM BOOKS FOR YOUNG READERS
New York London Toronto Sydney New Delhi

ATHENEUM BOOKS FOR YOUNG READERS
An imprint of Simon & Schuster Children's Publishing Division
1230 Avenue of the Americas, New York, New York 10020

For information about special discounts for bulk purchases, please contact
Simon & Schuster Special Sales at 1-866-506-1949 or business@simonandschuster.com.
The Simon & Schuster Speakers Bureau can bring authors to your live event.
For more information or to book an event, contact the Simon & Schuster Speakers Bureau
at 1-866-248-3049 or visit our website at www.simonspeakers.com.

Interior design by Karyn Lee
The text for this book was set in Celeste OT.
The illustrations for this book were rendered digitally.

Manufactured in the United States of America
0522 FFG
First Edition
2 4 6 8 10 9 7 5 3 1
Library of Congress Cataloging-in-Publication Data
Names: Senf, Lora, author. | Cáceres, Alfredo, 1983– illustrator.
Title: The Clackity / Lora Senf ; illustrated by Alfredo Cáceres.
Description: First edition. | New York : Atheneum Books for Young Readers, [2022] |
Series: A Blight Harbor novel | Audience: Ages 10–12. | Audience: Grades 4–6. |
Summary: To rescue her aunt from the ghost of a serial killer, twelve-year-old Evie Von
Rathe embarks on a journey into a strange world filled with hungry witches, ghosts, and a
story thief, all while trying to fulfill her deal with The Clackity.
Identifiers: LCCN 2021049653 | ISBN 9781665902670 (hardcover) | ISBN 9781665902687
(paperback) | ISBN 9781665902694 (ebook)
Subjects: CYAC: Ghosts—Fiction. | Witches—Fiction. | Serial murderers—Fiction. |
LCGFT: Novels. | Thrillers (Fiction)
Classification: LCC PZ7.1.S45 Cl 2022 | DDC [Fic]—dc23
LC record available at https://lccn.loc.gov/2021049653

To my parents,
Tom and Darlene,
who read to me and taught me to love words
and never tried too hard
to take away the scary books

PART ONE

Welcome to Blight Harbor

There was no shortage of otherworldly concerns in Blight Harbor, mainly because it was the seventh most haunted town in America (per capita).

Nearly everyone had a ghost living in their house or knew someone who did. And we all steered clear of the pair of seats in the movie theater that were always taken, and the streetlight on Derry Road that flickered if you stood under it at night and told a lie. There was the mirror in the town hall foyer that refused to reflect anything, which worked out just fine, because we were all pretty sure the mayor was descended from a long line of vampires on her maternal grandmother's side (although the mayor's husband was a regular guy named Steve). There were a hundred other things about Blight Harbor to worry about if you weren't used to them, but most of them were basically harmless. *Most* of them, anyway.

Which is why it was so strange that the only things bugging me this morning were the ordinary kind— as in (a) how late I was going to be to my summer job

volunteering at the library, and (b) how completely frustrating my aunt Desdemona was acting over breakfast.

It wasn't as if we didn't both have places to be. Aunt
Des had ghosts to dispel or poltergeists to ward off or
something, and I had to get to the library. But she insisted
we sit down for eggs and toast, which meant we were
both going to be late. Being late was on my list of things
that made my hands get all sweaty and my leg bounce
like it had a mind of its own. I mean, it was nowhere
near heights, but lateness was somewhere between tight
spaces and public speaking. Since I didn't like sweaty
hands and fidgety legs, I was pretty much never late for
anything.

So I sat waiting for the toast to pop, steaming just
like my eggs under their fogged-up frying pan lid, and
opened Friday's newspaper to the third page of the
Community section. There it was: top right-hand corner, like clockwork: Dear Desdemona: It's Not a Ghoul,
It's a Gift. Aunt D's advice column had been running
for a couple of months, and almost immediately it had
expanded from space available to twice weekly. Even
after living their whole lives in Blight Harbor, there
were still plenty of people who couldn't figure out how
to solve their supernatural problems on their own,
which meant there were plenty of letters and emails
coming in for Aunt D.

Over the top of my newspaper, Aunt D finally handed
me toast, soggy eggs, yogurt, and a cup of tea, all bal-
anced on a china plate that felt like it might fall apart
if a bell rang too loudly. At the sight of the weak tea, I

sighed dramatically. "Can I please have coffee?" Not that Des ever actually *let* me drink coffee, but it didn't stop me from trying.

Aunt D shook her head without even looking at me. "Evelyn, tea is much more interesting than coffee. A good cup of tea makes you more centered. Coffee just jangles your nerves and makes you unpleasant." Aunt D put a hand on my bouncing knee to calm it and raised a *See what I mean?* eyebrow at me. "Besides, you're too young."

"Well, you're like, fifty, so you shouldn't drink coffee because it will keep you up past your bedtime." It wasn't my best comeback, I know.

Aunt D turned to me in mock horror. "Evelyn Von Rathe! I will have you know I am turning forty-six next month. Which makes me nearly four times your age, which means . . ."

". . . you are four times wiser, and I should listen to your sage advice," I finished for her. I'd heard it a million times. I loved my aunt Des for lots of reasons, including how predictable she could be when she was in full-on Responsible-Adult-in-Charge mode. I also loved how easy it was to tease her about it.

"Correct." Aunt D sat down on the chair to my right. "How's the paper this morning?" Her big brown eyes actually sparkled in the morning sun. Sometimes she was like a cartoon character—a really annoying one who believed in hearty breakfasts.

"Hold on. I'm getting to the good part." I pulled the paper up higher so I didn't have to watch her watch me read.

The day's column went like this:

THE BLIGHT HARBOR HERALD

Dear Desdemona,

I'm in a bad spot and need your help! When I relocated to Blight Harbor, I was unaware of the town's reputation. Since moving into my new house, I've seen things shifting out of the corner of my eye, but they're gone when I try to look at them. I hear sounds, maybe people, moving in empty rooms. I feel breezes when the windows are closed. Desdemona, I live alone and have no pets, but I think I might have ghosts! I'm convinced my house is haunted. I am so scared I can't sleep, and I'm keeping lights on around the clock. Please help!

Sincerely,
Afraid of the Dark

Dearest Afraid,

All the events you describe are classic signs of a domestic haunting. Without having visited your home, I feel quite comfortable confirming that your house is, in fact, infested. Such signs lead me to believe there is more than one specter, and while I have no reason to assume your otherworldly housemates are threatening, I encourage you to research the history of your home and the land beneath it. If more than two murders occurred there, you may have something to be concerned about.

Please know this: there is no reason to fear the dark. Any paranormal being wishing to harm you in the nighttime is just as capable of doing so during the day. And electric lights make absolutely no difference. Night simply heightens our senses, and often our fear, making us more sensitive to the supernatural. Night is not to be dreaded any more, or less, than the day. I suggest a soothing cup of tea before bed, and perhaps leave one or two cups out for your roommates.

I hope this brings you great peace and allows you to sleep more soundly.

Welcome to Blight Harbor.

Kindest regards,

Desdemona Von Rathe

After I finished the column, I rested the paper on the table next to my breakfast. "It's pretty good." I was actually super proud of Des—she never seemed afraid of failing or of what other people might think about her. I kept hoping some of that confidence would rub off on me, but I was too irritated about running late to tell her any of that right then.

Aunt D's carefully shaped eyebrows nearly touched as concern scrunched her face. "Just 'pretty good'? Hm. Did I come off too stuffy or formal? I really wanted to address the seriousness of the concern without over-doing it. People can be so sensitive about their other-worldly conditions. . . ."

"No, no, no." Dang it. Not only had I hurt her feelings, but I was going to be extra late to the library if this kept on. My hands were getting clammy just thinking about it. "No, it was good. It was great, actually!" (I was really trying here.) "I'm sure Afraid feels tons better about mov-ing to Blight Harbor."

"Thank you, Evie." Aunt Desdemona smiled distract-edly as she put her long-nailed fingers in my hair. They got stuck as she tried to comb through. "Can we at least brush your mane before you go?"

"No time." I jumped up, shoving toast dipped in straw-berry yogurt into my mouth. I washed it all down with most of the tepid tea (secretly hoping D was right and that it *would* settle me). "Gotta get to the library before Lily freaks out." I slung my backpack over my shoulder, kissed my aunt on the top of her mass of dark curls, and headed for the front door.

"Women would kill for that copper hair of yours!" D called after me.

"Let me shave it and then they can have it!"

"No."

"Just underneath—the top can stay long!"

"No! You can be as weird as you want once you're thirteen."

"*You're* weird," I called as I slammed the door behind me.

I stopped in my tracks. Goodbyes were important, and that one was no good. I was already late and a few more seconds wouldn't make much difference.

I threw the door back open and didn't bother closing it—I wouldn't be in the house for long. I ran to Des, who was still sitting at the table, and wrapped my arms around her thin shoulders. "Love you, Aunt D."

She leaned her head against my cheek. "Love you too, sweet girl."

That was better.

We never parted without saying *I love you*. It was a rule. My rule. Because you could never know. You always think you're going to see someone again, but you really, truly never know. And of all the worries on my list, I guess that was the one that scared me the most.

The sky was as blue as a sky could get, and the morning sun was almost white, bleaching everything it touched. It would be a hot day, which was fine with me. I planned to spend most of it in the library, and the library was always the same temperature. I'd been volunteering there for the last year, usually a couple of days a week after school, and I planned to be there a lot more this summer because my best friend Maggie would be away until the end of August, traveling to France with her professor mom to study art. Maggie complained about it a lot—and I knew she'd miss me like I'd miss her—but I also knew she was excited to go. There were some other kids in town I knew,

and a couple I even liked, but honestly, I liked the library better.

The library was less than two miles from home and I was quick on my bike, so I made good time. I passed Maggie's house on the way and gave a quick wave to Florence, Maggie's house ghost, who was at the window, patiently waiting for our friend to come home. Florence had been in the house a lot longer than Maggie's family, and Maggie had been the ghost's favorite since she was born. I'd have to remember to stop by and check on her so she didn't get lonely.

Blight Harbor was extra sleepy this morning, but it was always a quiet town. At least the parts you could see during the day. Trees lined the streets in perfect, orderly rows, and all the redbrick buildings had bright white trim. Shops on the main street were named after Blight

Harbor residents—Janine's Hats and Gloves, Michael's Books, Mrs. Bradbury's Sweets and Teas—and everyone in town knew the people (or the ghosts of people) they were named for. It was just that kind of place. Which meant that everyone knew my aunt Desdemona and, by association, me. Plus, I was the girl who'd come to town four years ago when her parents died.

But disappearing is different from dying. My parents *disappeared*, and nobody could prove to me they died. I used to tell people that when I was younger, but I didn't bother anymore. I knew the difference, even if they didn't.

After my parents disappeared, I kind of freaked out for a while. Even four years later, I still got nervous. Worse than nervous, sometimes. But, mostly, there was a hollow, hurting place in me where my parents used to be. Aunt Des did her best to fill that place up with nice stuff. She was pretty good at it too. She said if I hid all my hurt away inside me, my insides would get moldy like wet laundry left in the washer for too long. Together, we worked hard to hang those things out to dry.

Sometimes I felt bad for feeling happy, like I wasn't supposed to have a good life until I knew where they were, or what had happened to them. Some days I didn't even think about my parents at all, and then I would feel bad about *that*. At least people had finally stopped looking at me with that *I'm so sorry for your loss* face. I knew they meant well, but having people pity me all the time was like an extra-heavy blanket I had to carry around everywhere I went.

I sped up on my bike a little, outpacing all the bad thoughts, and got myself back to the summer morning. Everyone I passed generally waved or nodded or called out as I rode by. School had been out for a few days, and since it was barely eight in the morning, I was pretty much the only kid on the street. Which suited me just fine. I wanted to get to the library in time to use the new computers for a few minutes before people started showing up.

At the library, I skidded to a stop and checked behind my bike, hoping I'd left a black trail of tire gunk on the sidewalk. I had, and that meant the day was off to a great start.

With my bike locked up, I took off my helmet and pulled my hair into a messy bun as I leaned against the heavy wooden front door of the Blight Harbor Town Library. Inside, cool air pooled around me and I took just a second to breathe in the library smells. Books and ink and the warm smell of dust—although the head librarian, Ms. Lily Littleknit, would have been put out with me for calling her library dusty.

Goose bumps climbed up my arms and the back of my neck. In my grey tank top and jeans, I was maybe a little underdressed for the chilly building. I pulled a thin black hoodie out of my backpack and zipped it up while looking around for Lily, who was easy to miss. She was all the same shade of tan, from her skin to her hair, and she usually wore clothes to match. I think she did it on purpose, dressing like an invisible person, so she could surprise you with her brains and her giant laugh, which was totally inappropriate for the "Shhh . . ." vibe of a library but fit her perfectly.

Lily was Aunt D's best friend, which made her like a second aunt to me. I loved her almost as much as D, and she made me nearly as crazy. Lily had been the first person in town other than Des to see *me* and not just all the bad stuff that had happened to me. The day I met her, she showed up at our house with a stack of books and some homemade shortbread cookies, which were basically my two favorite things. She'd looked into my eyes through her thick glasses and squeezed my arms gently, and even though we'd just met, I knew that squeeze meant *You're a strong one. You're going to be okay. I'm going to help make sure of it.* But she'd never looked at me with pity. Not once.

"Hey! Hey, Lily. Are you here?" I whisper-yelled into the center of the library. My voice got sucked up by the books and couches and carpets, but I imagined it still fluttered around in the highest corners of the pitched ceiling.

"Of course I'm here, Evelyn. And you're late. And stop yelling!" Lily yelled at me. Her voice was coming from the small periodicals section, right next to the new bank of computers. I followed it and found her sitting at one of eight monitors.

"Whatcha doing?" I dropped my backpack on the floor and sat at the computer next to her. Lily was leaning forward to read the computer screen, the monitor reflected in her glasses. She was wearing at least four shades of beige that day, which made her look like one of her famous baked goods.

"Reading the *Herald*." She didn't glance up from the screen but reached out and squeezed my arm. It was her way of saying, *Good morning. Nice to see you. Glad you're here.*

I looked at the short stack of newspapers waiting to be draped over wooden dowels to replace yesterday's editions. "Why not just read that one?"

"Easier on the computer. I can enlarge the text." If it weren't for her inch-thick glasses, I would forget Lily was half-blind. It seemed unfair that a woman about Aunt D's age who loved books more than people was slowly losing her eyesight, but she liked to say that she trusted medicine would catch up with her and that her eyes would get fixed before they got too bad. I liked to pretend I believed her, but it worried me all the same.

"Aunt D's column?"

The librarian turned to me with a bright smile. "Yes. You know, I was thinking. People must definitely believe she's a witch now. You know, the ones who didn't already." The idea seemed to amuse her. It just made me tired. I already stood out because of my parents, and thanks to Aunt D's sort-of newspaper fame. I really didn't want another reason.

"Yeah, and I'll be the witch's niece."

"Oh, sweetie." She patted me on the arm absently. "You already are."

She was right. Plenty of people in town thought Aunt Des was a witch. Not that it seemed to bother most of them. There were a few people—usually new to town (and who wouldn't stick around too long)—who would cross the street to avoid her, but mostly people were okay with it. Blight Harbor was the kind of town that was supposed to have a witch or two. And it did—it just wasn't Aunt D.

Lily had already powered up the machines, so all I had to do was log on and check some email. Aunt D's email, to be exact. She kept her calendar online as well, and I liked to know where she would be and what she'd be doing. Because sometimes she went weird places, and if she ever disappeared, I wanted to know where she'd headed last. I still had plenty to do in the library, but the work could wait. Tracking Des down came first. I was sure Lily would understand, even if she pretended to be grumpy about it.

Just the thought of Aunt D disappearing made my heart speed up and the place between my shoulder blades bunch into a tight little ball. I closed my eyes and took a few deep breaths. I was glad there wasn't anyone around but Lily to see me. Lily didn't count, because she knew me too well—and she knew what those deep, slow breaths meant. I knew she wouldn't say a thing about an *almost* panic attack—to me or Des. After all, almost wasn't the same as actually having one.

After Des, Lily was my second-best person. And honestly, after Des, I was hers, too. Knowing Lily was close by if I needed her made me feel a little calmer. Focusing always helped, so when my heart slowed down, I opened my eyes, fixed them on the computer screen, and got back to spying on Des. I wiped my now-sweaty hands on my jeans before putting them back on the keyboard.

Aunt D didn't have a regular job. She didn't need one. The inheritance she'd received from her own aunt and from my parents when they were declared legally dead wasn't massive, but it was enough for her—us—to live on if she was smart. And Aunt D was lots of things— weird, kind of spooky, and eccentric for sure—but not dumb. So instead of a real job, Aunt Des helped people out with their "otherworldly concerns." It was her way of describing ghosts and poltergeists and the like. And in Blight Harbor, there was always plenty of work to keep her busy. Moving to Blight Harbor had been a lot like being dropped in the middle of one of my favorite spooky books. The whole thing had taken some getting used to, but even when I was little, I loved living in a haunted town. Besides, most of the ghosts were perfectly nice.

I clicked past D's email and went straight to her calendar. I was surprised to see the whole day was blocked out with a dark purple box. I clicked on it, and there was nothing in the subject line. But the location was all I needed to see: *Abttr.* That was it. Five letters. But I knew exactly what they meant. She *knew* I checked her calendar—did Aunt D really think leaving the vowels out of a word was too tough a code for me to break? Or that I wouldn't want to come with her?

My heart started thumping again, but now it was because I was excited. I sometimes tagged along with Des on her missions, most recently when she was called to solve a haunted lamp problem (the solution was a lot of salt and a very hot oven—don't ask). Most of her jobs involved what she called *benign cases*—basically stuff that was more irritating than scary for the people involved. She didn't let me help with cases that could possibly get a tiny bit dangerous (even though they never really were). Which is probably why she didn't tell me about her plans for the day . . . which meant I was absolutely going because (a) I didn't want her being by herself, and (b) it was probably going to be cool (you should have seen what happened with the oven!).

I clicked back to her email, which was filled with the usual junk, plus a few new questions from her readers. There was nothing there that told me why she was going where she was going. But that was fine because I'd broken her terrible code, and I knew what I had to do next.

I signed out of Des's email and stood up, pushing my chair in too hard. The sound was a gunshot in the empty library. Thanks to the un-library-like noise, Lily jumped and scowled at me all at once. I gave her my best *I didn't mean to* face. "Sorry, gotta go."

"Evelyn, you just got here. And last night's books are waiting to be shelved." Lily pushed her heavy glasses up a bit to see me better.

"I know. I'm sorry. Promise I'll do it later. I just—I gotta go find Aunt Des and see what she's up to."

Lily Littleknit sighed. "You two are exactly alike, you know. Go. Find your aunt. Have an adventure. Take pictures of anything that might actually show up in a photograph. And please. You girls stay out of trouble."

I rode as fast as I could, shoulders hunched, face forward. I created my own wind in the otherwise still day. This time, when people smiled and waved, I ignored them. I had somewhere to be. This was my chance to investigate the abattoir.

I'd wanted to poke around the abandoned abattoir—which was just a fancy word for a slaughterhouse—since I'd come to Blight Harbor when I was eight. Aunt Desdemona didn't have many rules—not serious ones, anyway—but the old slaughterhouse was completely, totally off-limits, especially since it reminded everyone in town of Blight Harbor's most infamous villain. Which meant I really, really wanted to check it out. I loved weird old places—fortunately, the town was full of them—and wanted nothing more than to poke around and look for secrets. But if Aunt D, who wasn't scared of anything, didn't want me there, I figured she had her reasons.

Still.

Aunt D was going to be at the abattoir all day, which meant this was my chance to finally explore the place. As curious as I was, I wasn't about to go there alone, and

Maggie refused to go with me (I'd tried to convince her more than once). I thought about calling but decided to surprise Aunt D instead. It would be harder for her to say no if I was already there.

The library was on the east side of town, and the abattoir was on the far west, on the outskirts of a quiet neighborhood. All together, it was probably a five-mile trip. I stopped only once to strip off my hoodie and shove it back into my bag. The day was heating up in a hurry.

As I got close, I could see Aunt D's small black SUV parked on the dirt road beside the slaughterhouse. I pulled up behind the car, tires kicking dust into the air. I left my bike there and walked into the long grass in front of the building to get a better view.

I'd never been this close to the abattoir before. In the bright light of day, it was kind of pretty. The building was three stories tall, all faded wood and grey brick. The doors and most of the windows were gone, but it didn't look decrepit. Abandoned, for sure, but not decrepit. If anything, the old building looked strong. Like it would stand there another hundred years, whether anyone wanted it to or not.

It looked—defiant. Sometimes places are like people and have their own personalities. They can be warm or cold. Friendly or mean. The abattoir was intimidating. It made me feel really small, like I could get lost just standing in its shadow.

I stepped toward the gaping front entrance. When it was new and people still worked there, it would have been closed by two enormous doors, but they were long gone. Once I reached the threshold, my eyes widened, and I had to tip my head back to take in how huge the building really was. It was bigger than the gym at my school for sure, and a lot taller. Anything that had once been in this building had long ago been stripped out. Only a dirt floor and the occasional concrete block remained.

Sunlight streamed in through the holes and the windows. A chilly breeze came from somewhere inside the abattoir, which was odd because the day was so warm. I shivered, partly from being surprised by the cool air and partly from being a little creeped out. There was no garbage or junk anywhere. You'd expect kids to hang out in old buildings like this, maybe even throw late-night parties, but the place was pristine. The whole thing just felt off. My Spidey sense was tingling, the one that said, *Look out! Danger! There's someone right around the corner!*

But there was no sign that anyone ever came in here.

Except Aunt Desdemona.

She stood at the far wall, close enough to touch it, her back turned to me. With her black summer dress and pale skin, she blended into the dancing light and shadows. She was studying something, maybe the scuff marks that covered the grey cement on the back wall of the room. Ten feet up, just over her left shoulder, was an enormous metal shaft jutting three feet out of the wall. It looked tall enough that I'd be able to stand up straight in the middle of it with room to spare. I had a feeling it was a doorway—a doorway to nowhere good.

I was feeling a little guilty for showing up where I wasn't supposed to be and was trying to figure out if I should call out to Des or wait until I got closer to announce I was there. It turned out I didn't need to decide.

"Hi, Evelyn." Her exasperated voice carried in the emptiness. "I should've known you'd come."

"Sorry . . ." I trailed off. I wasn't *very* sorry, but it seemed like the right thing to say. I stood in the entrance, waiting to be yelled at or sent home. Aunt D wasn't much for yelling, but, like I said, she didn't have very many rules, and I'd broken a pretty big one by showing up at the abattoir.

"Well, come on. You're here, so you might as well see this. Be careful not to step in any drains."

Drains? Of course. It was a slaughterhouse. There would be drains. I shuddered, not wanting to think about why drains were needed in a place like that.

A few yards into the building, the smell caught up with me. It was the earthy animal smell of a barn, and I immediately thought of livestock at the county fairs I'd visited when I was little, all the animals in cramped pens just lying there, disinterested, as the kids mooed or poked at them through the gates. But there was another smell just under that, and it was rotten and sick. Despite the bright blue day and the breeze and Aunt D being on the other side of the room, for the first time I wasn't so sure I wanted to be in the abattoir after all. That hard little ball was back between my shoulders, and I wiggled them back and forth, trying to loosen it up. If my hands kept sweating, I was going to rub a hole in my jeans trying to dry them off.

As I approached her, I could see what my aunt was

looking at. What I had thought were scuff marks on the wall were actually birds. Someone had drawn dozens of birds—maybe a hundred—across the entire back wall of the slaughterhouse. Some looked close, others far off in the distance. They were all black silhouettes, and all in flight. Not crows or ravens, but something smaller. Sparrows or finches, maybe. They were beautiful and terrible all at the same time. Birds didn't belong in a place like this. I know it sounds weird, but I wanted to set them free.

Despite the wide-open space, I was beginning to feel claustrophobic. The place was empty, but it *felt* full. Like when you walk into a vacant room but you just *know* someone was there a second before. Usually that feeling goes away pretty quick, but in the abattoir, the feeling got stronger. It made the air thick and hard to breathe—or maybe that last part was just me.

"Who would do that?" I spoke quietly when I reached Aunt D.

"I don't know," she almost whispered. She adjusted the small black purse that hung on her shoulder, reached out, and touched one of the birds. I resisted an urge to pull her hand away from the wall and not let it go until we were through the front door and back in the sun.

Instead I just said, "Don't."

Aunt D turned and considered me with serious eyes. "Why not?"

"I don't know. I just—I just don't like it. They shouldn't be here."

She nodded. "I agree. What I want to know is how they got here. I've rubbed at them, picked at them, tried to feel for their edges." She showed me her hands, front and back. They were dusty, but unstained by ink or paint or anything else.

I drew up as close to one of them as I dared to get a better look. I still didn't want to touch anything. "Burned, maybe?"

"I thought so too. But no. No charcoal or ash."

Focusing on something usually made me feel better when I was nervous, so I kept looking, searching for clues. The birds were part of the wall, but there were places where time had worn them down, revealing the concrete beneath. "They've been here a really long time. So, who knows?" I supposed they were strange, but compared to other stuff—like that time we had to spend a whole day telling jokes and playing loud pop music in a house because the radio wouldn't stop turning itself on and playing sad, old-fashioned music, even when it was unplugged—I couldn't figure out why they made me feel so uneasy. This *was* Blight Harbor, after all.

Desdemona shook her head. When she spoke, she spoke to me. But she also spoke to someone else. Herself maybe, or the birds, or the emptiness filling that awful place. "No, Evie. They weren't here yesterday. Which is why I'm here today."

I didn't know what to say to that. I didn't even know if I believed it. It seemed like no one ever came here, so maybe it was just that no one had noticed. My attention was again drawn to the giant metal duct just to the left of us, the one sticking out of the wall into nothing. "What *is* that thing?"

Aunt D looked up at the shaft, then back at me. "That's where they would stun and bleed the animals before"—she gestured vaguely to the rest of the massive room—"before they did everything else they did to them here."

"Okay. Got it. Don't wanna know any more." I didn't mind spooky stuff, but this place wasn't regular Blight Harbor spooky. If anything, it was sad. And gross. I was beginning to seriously appreciate just how wrong the abattoir felt. It was no wonder kids never hung out here.

Then I noticed something else, and I looked all around the room just to be sure. The building was surrounded by grass and bushes and trees. Outside, I could hear birds and crickets and what I thought might even be frogs. But inside? Nothing. Not a sparrow in the rafters or a spider in the corner. The building should have been full of wild and crawling things taking advantage of all that space. But it wasn't. Not a single living thing existed inside except me and my aunt Desdemona. It made the little hairs on my arms stand up, and my insides got all heavy like I'd had a big glass of cement to drink.

"Can we go?" I could feel familiar panic filling me up like cold water.

"You can go. I need to stay for a while."

And then suddenly the smell in the room was overpowering as everything seemed to close in, fold up around me. My breath got quick and shallow, and no matter how hard I tried, I couldn't get enough air. My heart tried to crawl up in my throat to escape. Hot tears filled my eyes, and my voice came out like broken glass. "No. No, Aunt D.

You have to leave with me and come home. You can't be here all by yourself anymore. Please, okay? Let's just go. We can talk about it at home. You can tell me all about it."

When she turned my way, she looked in my direction but didn't *look* at me. Her gaze was fixed on something behind me, over my shoulder.

I spun around. As anxious as I was, I couldn't help but try to catch a glimpse of whatever had caught Aunt D's attention.

There was nothing there. Just a broken-out window and bright green leaves on the other side of the wall and deep black shadows in the corner. Then Des's eyes sharpened and stared hard into mine. "Okay. Let's go. Now. You first."

So we did. And I was glad.

Thinking back on it, I should have known something spooked her, too, but I was too busy trying not to freak out to give it any more thought. Too busy not panicking to remember to ask her what she saw when she looked over my shoulder.

The air outside was summer clean, and my first thought was that I would need to wash my hair and my clothes—maybe twice—to get the smell of the place out. But outside I could breathe, and the worst of the panic made its way out of me and found somewhere else to go.

When I walked far enough away from the abattoir that I was out of its shadow, I turned to look at it. The hot day wasn't doing much for my goose bumps, but I did feel safer being next to Des and under the blue sky and yellow morning sun. There was no way around it—the abattoir had scared me, though I couldn't put my finger on exactly why. It was the empty-but-too-full feeling, and the way those poor birds were trapped inside. Which was silly, because they were just drawings, but something can be silly and true at the same time.

Then I got to thinking about the sort-of-scared, sort-of-determined look in D's eyes when she told me we were leaving. And the edge to her voice when she told me to go first. And that smell. And those dark, dark shadows that seemed all piled up in the corner . . .

I jumped when Aunt D put her hand on my shoulder. She smiled at me, but it was as weak as her morning tea. Then she headed toward the car, me right on her heels.

As we loaded up my bike in the back of the SUV, she told me, "Your shoes come off before you go into the house. Mine, too. We might have to throw them away. I don't like to think about what that floor has soaked up."

Apparently, Aunt D was thinking almost the same thing I was about getting clean after our trip to the abattoir.

As we started toward home, Aunt Des said we both needed tea and naps. I didn't want either. I just wanted my day to get back to normal.

"Can you please take me back to the library?"

She glanced over at me as she drove. Her eyes were hidden behind giant black sunglasses, but she sucked in her cheeks and clenched her jaw. I knew the look. It was her *Evelyn, I don't think that's a good idea* face. "Evelyn, I don't think that's a good idea."

Nailed it. "I'm fine."

"Are you really? You haven't had a spell in a long time. You seemed . . . close."

She didn't like to call them panic attacks, even though that's what they were. I mean, my counselor called them panic attacks, and he knew his stuff. I couldn't care less what we called them, as long as they stayed away.

"I'm good. I swear. That place was just . . . gross and weird and smelled disgusting." It wasn't a very good description, but I couldn't find the right words. For lots of little reasons that would have sounded silly if I'd said them out loud, the place was terrible. And scary. And, I was pretty sure, dangerous.

"It *is* gross and weird and it *does* smell disgusting. Which is why I want you to stay away from it."

"Are you going back? Because of the birds?"

"I don't know. Probably, yes. But not today."

Not ever, if I have anything to say about it.

"Why birds?" I asked.

Desdemona sighed, thinking. "Birds are powerful things. Big birds are powerful all by themselves, but little birds are different. Little birds like those sparrows are powerful in groups. And there must have been, what, a hundred of them on that wall?"

I nodded. "Yeah. At least."

"Two things I'm thinking about." She held up two elegant fingers, dropping them one at a time as she spoke. "One, sparrows are an old, old symbol of protection. Two, a flock of sparrows can fight off something much larger when they work together."

"So, do you think they're protecting something, or fighting something?"

Aunt Des stopped at a red light. The SUV's blinker told me she was turning in the direction of the library. She took off her sunglasses and looked at me hard. Her dark eyes were tired and worried. No cartoon sparkle now. "Maybe a little of both. Maybe they're keeping something from getting out."

"John Jeffrey Pope?" Most ghosts were harmless, but if there was a ghost in Blight Harbor that people were scared of, it was Pope. No one had actually seen him since he died, but that didn't make the possibility any less frightening. The town was strange for sure, but it wasn't *bad*. Pope had been more than bad when he'd been alive. He'd been downright evil, and if he was going to haunt a place, the abattoir was as good a bet as any.

Desdemona made a disgusted noise in the back of her throat and put her glasses back on. "If that creature were there, we'd know it by now. No, it's something else."

We drove the rest of the way to the library in silence. I guess we both had a lot to think about, but not a whole lot to say.

After we arrived at the front of the building, I went to the back of the car and got my bike. Then I went to the driver's side and opened the door. I grabbed Des's hand and squeezed it, and she squeezed back, which meant I had her attention and she was really, truly listening. "Do you promise you aren't going back?" I couldn't quite shake the *wrong* feeling I had about the abattoir. My bones felt heavy from the weight of it, and my stomach was filling up with clanking glass marbles of dread. I needed to be sure she was safe, and Aunt D never broke a promise.

Desdemona leaned toward me so I could see her eyes. She wasn't humoring me. "I promise I am not going back to that wretched place today."

"Good. You're weird, but I love you." I kissed her on the cheek.

"You make me crazy, but I love you, too." Desdemona grabbed both sides of my face and kissed the top of my head. "Say hi to that old witch Lily for me."

I smiled. "I will. And I'll tell her you said that."

"Please do, darling."

And then the window was up, and she was gone.

Back in the library, I found Lily and told her about the abattoir and the birds and the weird feeling inside the building. I didn't mention my almost panic attack. Aunt D was already worried; I didn't need the two of them on the phone worrying together. Sometimes they were like two crows squabbling over the same bug, which could be funny. Except when I was the bug. Then it was just exhausting. "Oh, and Des said to say hi and she called you an old witch."

Lily rolled her eyes. "Tell her I said hi, and that she's a second-rate fortune-teller. That should piss her off."

I laughed too loud for the library, and Lily shushed me, even though it was her fault. After the abattoir, the library was nice—safe and familiar and predictable. I took a deep breath, filling myself with the dusty, inky, book-scented air, then letting it out slow and steady.

I spent the rest of the late morning shelving books and dusting fixtures. By lunchtime, the library was in good order, even by Lily's standards. We sat at the reference desk eating berries and sliced cheese and crackers. The berries came from Lily's garden. I recognized most of them, but a few were new to me.

"Currants," Lily said, holding up the tiniest red gems close to her thick glasses. "And these are gooseberries." The translucent pink orbs had a tinge of green to them. They were tart and sweet and wonderful.

I ate in silence, knowing a Lily Lesson was coming. Even if I would never admit it to her, Lily was the smartest person I knew, and I loved it when she taught me random stuff. Thanks to her, I knew all about which animals to pay attention to if you wanted to know how bad a storm would be (cats), which plants could help you figure out what direction you were going (oak trees were the ones to look for, but lots of other trees would do). The best was when we spent almost an hour on deer poop—er, droppings—while Lily explained how they helped predict particularly bad winters (don't ask).

"Currants look an awful lot like holly berries. But holly berries are brighter, redder. And it doesn't take many to kill a kiddo or an animal. Gooseberries have an evil twin as well—mistletoe. Mistletoe berries won't kill you, but they'll make you wish you were dead." Lily held her stomach and made an embarrassing face.

"Gross," I said.

"You bet. Homework for this afternoon—look up all four berries on the computer so you know the difference."

"Then can I mess around on the internet?"

"Sure. Just don't look up anything you'd be embarrassed for Pastor Mike to see." Pastor Mike was one of the half-dozen pastors in Blight Harbor, and that was just counting the Protestants. Most people in Blight Harbor went to some kind of church or temple or synagogue. Living in Blight Harbor, it was hard not to believe in *something*. And, honestly, some folks were just hedging their bets. When you lived in the seventh most haunted town in America (per capita), it was just smart. I for sure believed in an afterlife, and God, but I wasn't so sure about what church He would go to on Sunday mornings.

"Gross."

"You get more articulate every day." Lily squeezed my arm and got up to answer the ringing phone.

After googling the berries—*twenty holly berries can kill a dog*—I looked around to see Lily back at her desk reading a large-print copy of the latest bestseller. The way she chewed on her thumbnail told me it must be good, and that she'd be reading until a patron came in or called. Lily was distracted, which was exactly how I wanted her. Lily and Des bickered a lot, but one thing they agreed on was that I shouldn't get "bogged down in dark stuff." And that was exactly what I was about to do.

I hunched over the monitor and typed *Blight Harbor John Jeffrey Pope* into the search bar. The results came back before my finger was off the enter key. I scrolled down until I found an entry I'd read a bunch of times before.

Pope was notorious in Blight Harbor. Living in a place like Blight Harbor meant you had to love history— or at least accept it—since so much of it just kept hanging around. But Pope was different. He'd been gone for a hundred years, but what he had done was like a stain on our town's story. We didn't study him in school or anything, but we might as well have, considering how much everyone knew about him. Blight Harbor wasn't afraid of ghosts, but people who made other people into ghosts were a whole different matter.

Basically, Pope was our resident boogeyman.

Even though I already knew there was a connection between him and the abattoir because he had worked there (that was common knowledge), I thought I might be able to figure out if Pope had something to do with the bird drawings on the wall. On the drive back to the library, Aunt Des had said she didn't think they were connected, but I wasn't convinced. Like I said, I loved exploring places, looking for their secrets. And maybe the abattoir had a secret even Des didn't know.

I clicked on a link and began reading.

Pope, Jonathan Jeffrey (1887–?).
American.
Suspected serial killer.
Active years (assumed), 1919–1921.

The black-and-white photo in the middle of the page was pretty well known around town. It showed a group of five brothers. They were all handsome in an old-fashioned way, with square jaws and eyes half-shut from the sun. They all looked serious. All of them except the second man from the left. With sandy hair falling over one eye, he was the most handsome of the group but smaller and thinner than the rest, and the only one who was smiling. His grin was big and toothy and charming. It gave me the creeps. The photo had been edited so that he stood out a little brighter than the others. The caption read: *J. J. Pope, 1919. Photo courtesy of Pope family archives.*

It seemed wrong that he was nice-looking. It made

him scarier, somehow. It wasn't fair that evil people should get to hide behind wide, friendly smiles. It was a trap. And according to history, that trap must have worked.

I kept reading.

> *Jonathan (John) Jeffrey Pope was born in the small town of Blight Harbor and resided there until his disappearance in 1921. It is believed he was responsible for the murders of upward of a dozen people beginning in 1919. The likely murders are classified as unsolved missing persons cases, as the bodies were never found. A slaughterhouse worker, Pope is believed to have disposed of his victims in his place of employment. Some forensic evidence was recovered, primarily human fingers and toes, but the technology of the era was not sophisticated enough to positively identify . . .*

"Evie!" Lily yelled my name and I instinctively clicked off the screen. Guilt poured over me like sticky molasses, even though *technically* I wasn't doing anything wrong. But I knew Aunt Des wouldn't like me spending a bunch of time reading about Pope. She'd think I was worrying about today (which I guess I kind of was). I also knew Lily told Aunt D almost everything, so I figured I'd have to do some more research on my phone after I went to bed.

"Yeah?" I got up from the computer, stretched, and walked to the desk, where Lily sat with her book open, the pages weighted down with a stapler.

"A few more books to shelve, then I want you heading out. Desdemona called. She needs you home early tonight."

"Um, okay. Why?"

"No idea. Didn't ask."

But I knew. It was because of today. The abattoir. And my "spell." Aunt D wanted me home before dark, even though that was still hours away. She wasn't worried about what might be creeping around town. After all, it wasn't a full moon or the summer solstice or even the fourth of May in an odd-numbered year (now *that* was a night to stay inside). She was worried about *me*.

I put away the small stack of books that had grown on the desk over the last hour. I saved the thick collection of Brothers Grimm fairy tales (maybe my favorite stories of all time) and the John Bellairs books for last. *The House with a Clock in Its Walls. The Mummy, the Will, and the Crypt. The Curse of the Blue Figurine.* I had read those books a hundred times when I was younger. Someone had good taste.

On my way out the door, Lily handed me a small plastic container still cold from the fridge in the staff workroom. "Currants and gooseberries," she said. "Don't tell Desdemona. She'll eat them all."

I smiled and dropped the snacks into my backpack. I figured with my luck I'd forget they were there and remember them next week when my bag started to stink.

I thanked Lily, gave her a side hug, and went out the front door of the library.

The air was still and hot. Heavy. As I rode through town, the streets were quiet. Everyone who could be inside was. Blight Harbor was a hunkered-down thing, shielding itself from the sun until evening came and it could breathe again.

When I got home, I saw Aunt D's shoes on the front porch and remembered to take mine off before going inside. The soles of my all-black Converse high-tops were a little rusty-looking, but otherwise they seemed okay. I walked in the front door and dropped my bag on the floor.

"Aunt Des! I'm home!"

"In the kitchen," she answered. I followed her voice to the big table in the middle of the room. She was having tea again, but iced and sweet this time. She poured me a glass as I sat down. She didn't waste any time. "Are you okay?"

"You mean from earlier? I'm fine. I got it under control."

"I know. And I'm proud of you. But what if something big had happened—something more than birds on a wall and a nasty smell? Would you have been okay then?"

I blushed. I was embarrassed, and kind of angry, because Aunt D had a point, and I didn't want to talk about it. We'd talked about this stuff a thousand times already.

"I don't know." We didn't lie to each other, Des and me.

Des looked at me for a few seconds. Long enough to make me look away before turning back and matching her stare. I saw worry and something that might have been fear in her dark, dark eyes. I didn't like it. I didn't like it one bit that something was scaring my fearless aunt.

Finally she raised her glass and sipped, then asked, "What makes you feel brave?"

"I don't know." It was a weird question.

"Okay. Trying again. You dress tough. Does it make you feel tough?" She meant my uniform of black and grey shirts and blue jeans. Black All Stars in hot weather, big black boots in cooler months.

"Yeah, I guess. Yeah. But I don't dress tough, really."

"Yes, you do."

Aunt Des let the words hover in the air between us like hummingbirds.

My eyes started to tear up, threatening to spill over. Pretending to be tough was one thing; talking about it was another. "It makes me feel invincible." I started rambling before I knew what I was going to say. "It makes me feel strong. And hard, like nothing can hurt me. And, yeah, brave. And maybe it makes other people think I'm those things. And if *they* think I am, then I am."

I thought Aunt Des would shake her head and argue with me. Instead she nodded. "You're right. Sometimes we are who other people think we are." After a pause, she said, "Come on. We're doing this before I change my mind."

Desdemona got up from the table and walked up the

narrow stairs to our second floor. I followed her into the bathroom we shared in the mornings, where she had already put a tall stool in front of the mirror that hung over the sink.

"Sit down." She gestured at the seat.

When I sat, she began brushing my hair, gentle except when she had to fight with knots and tangles. The whole thing was a little weird. Aunt D always wanted to brush my hair, but I couldn't remember the last time she actually had. My leg started bouncing like it was keeping time with my heart.

"Des, what . . . ?"

"Shhh. I don't know what I'm doing and you're making me nervous." She took a comb and began separating my hair an inch above my ears. She pulled the top half into a high bun and left the rest hanging. It wasn't until she plugged in the clippers that I knew what she was about to do.

My hands got sweaty, but it was a good kind of sweaty.

"But you said—"

"I know what I said. Now be quiet. I'll do my best, but we might have to take you to Miss Stephanie to get it cleaned up." And with that, Aunt D began to shave my head. I'd spent ages begging for this haircut. I was afraid to say anything, much less move, for fear she'd change her mind.

When she was finished, I inspected the results. She'd done a good job. It was pretty even, and the lines were mostly straight. When I let my hair down, only a bit of the shaved sides peeked out.

"It's perfect." It was the haircut I'd been bugging her about for months. The haircut she had refused to let me have. And it *was* perfect. I stood up and hugged her hard, careful not to step on the snakes of dark red hair covering the bathroom floor.

Aunt Des squeezed me back. "I can't believe I just did that to your beautiful hair." There was a smile in her voice when she said it.

I pulled what was left of my hair back up in a bun, admiring my new look while she swept the bathroom. I wished Maggie was around so I could show her. She'd flip out, and before long we'd be scheming how to get her mom to let her dye her dark hair violet. I started to leave the bathroom, thinking I might message her, but Aunt Des stopped me.

"Not quite done. Sit down." She'd already given me the best surprise, so I wasn't about to tell her no to anything else she had planned.

She pulled out a black eyeliner pencil from a drawer and tapped my eyebrows with her fingers, telling me silently to close my eyes. I did and felt the gentle drag and pull of the waxy pencil. When she was done, I opened my eyes and took in the girl in the mirror across from me. She had green eyes lined in black, and a fresh undercut. She was strong and tough and ready for anything. I couldn't believe she was me. She was exactly who I wanted to be.

"One more thing."

"I don't want to wear lipstick."

"Yeah, no. You're not even thirteen until September.

And you're also not wearing the eyeliner to school next year. Just be quiet."

Aunt Des opened a box she'd placed on the bathroom counter. From it she pulled a long, heavy-linked silver necklace. When she wrapped it around my neck twice, it fit almost like a choker. It weighed a ton, but it felt good.

I looked like a badass.

Aunt Des read my mind and smiled. Some of her cartoon sparkle was back. "Yeah, now *that* is a tough look. You like it?"

I nodded. I liked it a lot. I loved it. I was so happy it hurt a little, and I was shaking just a tiny bit. It was weird how good things and bad ones could hurt for such different reasons. I knew it was just a haircut and some eyeliner, but it made me feel like I was wearing armor. Tears burned my eyes, but I refused to let them slip out. Crying would have ruined the effect.

"When you get scared, or worried, or start to panic, I want you to remember that girl." Desdemona pointed hard at the familiar stranger in the mirror. "Because you *are* that girl. Makeup and a terrible haircut just make it easier to see. Okay?"

I nodded, not trusting my voice.

"You can keep the eyeliner, but don't wear it to the library or I'll never hear the end of it from Lily. But the necklace. The necklace I want you to wear, okay? It's smart to wear a bit of real silver in a place like Blight Harbor. Besides, it suits you."

"Thank you, Des." I kissed my aunt on the cheek, which wasn't much of a stretch since I was almost as tall as her. Then I wrapped my arms around her and gave her the biggest squeeze I could—which might have been too big, because she let out kind of a whooshing sound. She deserved that hug. Aunt D had been doing stuff like this for me ever since I moved in with her. She wasn't one of my parents, but she worked really hard to be my family.

"You know you're the best aunt, right?" I asked her.

She took my face in her hands and looked at me with shiny eyes (Aunt D was a crier). "Sweet girl, I don't know if that's true or not, but I promise I'll always be the best I can be."

I kissed her again, then let her go and ran off to message Maggie.

I spent the rest of the afternoon in the house, reading books and hiding from the heat. I kept running my hands along the new short little hairs on the back of my head, and more than once I found myself in front of a mirror. Dinner was whatever cold stuff we picked out of the fridge. The evening slipped by in a lazy, summertime sort of way, and when bedtime rolled around, I was worn out. I finally closed my book.

Aunt Des was in her favorite chair, feet tucked under her, reading a horror novel with a cheesy cover (which I fully intended to borrow from her later), when I went to kiss her good night.

"Good night, sweet girl. And take the makeup off before bed, okay? It's bad for your skin to leave it on."

"I will. Promise."

I was on my way up the stairs when Desdemona called softly, "Evie?"

I poked my head down to see her. "Yeah?"

"You are the bravest, strongest, smartest girl I know. And I love you more than anything, okay?" I was going to say something sarcastic to her, but the look on her face stopped me.

"I love you, too, Aunt Des."

"I'm glad. Good night, baby."

"Good night." I closed my bedroom door, the house quiet and peaceful on the other side.

If I had known what would happen next, I'd have gone back down for another hug.

I'd forgotten to close the window shade the night before, so my bedroom was hot when I woke up. In fact, it was the heat that woke me. Bright, midmorning sun cut across the room and rested on my neck and shoulders like a second blanket.

Aunt Des usually made me get up "at a civil hour," even on summer weekends. So when my eyes focused enough to see the white sheet of paper on my nightstand, I went on high alert. Suddenly wide awake, heart pounding, I snatched the paper off the small table and began to read. It didn't take long.

> *Evie,*
> *There is something I need to do. I have*
> *to try to fix something before it gets worse*
> *and I can't fix it anymore. If I'm not home*
> *by dinner, go to Lily's house.*
> *Don't try to follow me. I'll be back as*
> *soon as I can.*
> *I love you, sweet girl.*

Love,
D
P.S. Be strong and brave if you have to,
but be smart first.

I knew.

I knew immediately where she was. Desdemona had gone back to the abattoir. She had kept her promise and hadn't gone back yesterday, but technically this was a new day.

And she was crazy if she thought I wasn't going to follow her, to help her do whatever it was she had to do. Since Mom and Dad disappeared, the idea of losing anyone else terrified me. And Aunt Des was my *everyone* else. Everyone I had left.

My hands were trembling when I grabbed my phone off the nightstand and dialed D's number. It rang and rang until her voice mail picked up.

I tried again. Voice mail.

I threw my phone onto my bed.

I felt the familiar fingers of panic creeping up the back of my neck. Those fingers dug their way into my throat. My heart and lungs worked too hard and too fast, and I began to shiver like it wasn't almost a hundred degrees outside. I told myself maybe D was just busy. Maybe she was driving and couldn't answer. I made up all the non-scary maybes I could. If I didn't get it under control soon, the trembling would turn into full-body shakes and I wouldn't be able to get down our steep stairs to the first floor, much less on my bike and out to the abattoir to help her.

To save her, maybe.

I ran quaking hands through my hair. I'd forgotten about my new haircut until right then. Remembering the girl in the mirror wasn't enough to make the anxiety go away, but it was enough to get me moving.

I threw on clean clothes—a black tank top and jeans. Then, giving myself five minutes max, I went into the bathroom and splashed water on my face. I twisted what was left of my long hair into a knot high up on my head. I found last night's eyeliner and put it on as best I could with still-shaking hands. I focused and focused and calmed down a little. The eyeliner wasn't perfect, but when I smudged it a little with my fingertip, it looked better. The silver necklace once again wrapped around my neck, I looked critically in the mirror. I expected to feel silly in the daylight with the new hair and makeup.

I didn't.

I looked like a warrior. And I felt . . . defiant. The word had fit the abattoir yesterday, and it fit me today. I liked defiant a whole lot better than terrified.

My heart was beating hard, but now the pounding was from adrenaline instead of panic.

I went back to my room and shoved D's note into my backpack. Downstairs, out the front door, All Stars on my feet, on my bike, and I was gone.

Desdemona wasn't going to do anything stupid. Not without me, anyway.

Aunt D's black SUV was parked in the same place she'd left it the day before. I dropped my bike behind the car, not bothering with the kickstand.

I tore off my helmet and threw it to the ground as I ran to the gaping, doorless hole. I didn't know how I'd seen anything pretty in the old building the day before. The sun was almost directly overhead and there were no shadows. The slaughterhouse stood raw and exposed in the mean light, its broken windows staring like too many empty eyes.

I stopped at the entrance, just like I had the previous day, not sure what to do. But if Desdemona was in the abattoir, I needed to get her out. It wasn't something I felt, it was something I *knew*. I stepped reluctantly over the threshold and into the slaughterhouse.

The odor inside the building had grown worse, both heavier and sharper. The abattoir no longer smelled like the echoes of what it had once been, but like it had decades ago, not long after they stopped bringing the animals there to die. And it was hot inside, hotter than the day beyond its walls.

At first I couldn't see my aunt. For a second, I was so relieved that all my muscles relaxed and I breathed out some of the thick, liquid weight that had filled my lungs. Maybe she'd just gone out to the field behind the building, or to a neighboring house. I reached for my phone to call Des again, then remembered it was back home on my bed where I'd thrown it. It didn't matter. I'd find her and then we'd be home and done with this place.

The echoey sound of feet on sheet metal filled the air, hollow footfalls coming from somewhere overhead. Then I noticed the ladder, the one that hadn't been there the day before. It rested up against the edge of the stun shaft high on the back wall. And there, in the shadows, I could see Desdemona, almost invisible in the gloom of the shaft. Her back was turned to me. Her narrow shoulders were squared and brave, but her right hand fidgeted nervously at her side.

In the far corner of the abattoir, on the other side of the back wall below the shaft, the shadows were unnaturally dark. And they shifted and churned. Something was there. Something else was in the abattoir with my aunt.

"Des!" I screamed it. "Get out!"

I couldn't see her face, but the terror in my aunt's voice told me everything I needed to know. She didn't scream at me, or even yell. Instead her voice came out as a wailing sort of moan.

"Baby. Run."

And I did.

I ran as fast as I'd ever run.

But I didn't run away from the abattoir.

I sprinted as fast and as hard as I could across that huge, horrible room toward my aunt, because not losing her was more important—was *bigger*—than anything I was afraid of in there.

Within seconds, I could see I hadn't run fast enough. I stopped in my tracks and craned my neck up toward the shaft. I tried to convince myself that what I was seeing couldn't be right. Where there had been darkness in the stun shaft only moments before, now bright summer light streamed through the opening.

Desdemona was gone. My aunt, my best person, my *everyone* was gone.

But the thing in the churning shadows was still there.

Sweat poured down my neck and chest, but I was cold to my bones. My heart beat so fast it felt like it was vibrating, like it had sprouted hummingbird wings and would fly out of my chest and chase after my aunt if it had half a chance. My breath was just a shallow whine. I backed away from the shadows, trying to put as much space as possible between the darkness and me. As I moved back, my mind raced, and I did everything I could to focus, focus, *focus*—I needed to get to the ladder and up to the shaft and after Des. But that meant getting closer to the shadows and whatever was in them.

I took another step back, but my foot kept going down when it should have landed on solid, dirt-covered ground. I fell backward, twisted to catch myself, and landed on my side and on my backpack. I had stepped in one of the drains Aunt D had warned me about yesterday, back when I thought the abattoir was *pretty*. Disgusted—at myself and at whatever was still in the drain—I yanked my foot out. I did a quick check to verify that nothing hurt. Somehow, I'd managed to avoid twisting my ankle.

I scooted backward, still making space between myself and the shadows in the corner. They shifted and stirred, but they didn't approach me. Watching closely, I could see shades of charcoal and black, and could almost make out a figure, but whatever it was wasn't familiar enough for my mind to make sense of it.

I changed direction and edged toward the ladder. By the time I reached the rungs, I was so freaked out I was basically numb, but I couldn't look away from the shadows. If whatever was in there wanted to hurt me, I figured there wasn't much I could do about it. So I kept moving, because it was either that or stop and freeze completely. I had frozen before in far less terrifying situations.

I stood, placing both of my sweaty, shaking hands on rusty metal. I wasn't sure my body would even work well enough to get me up the rungs, but I had to keep moving. I had to try.

When I touched the ladder, two things happened at once.

A thrumming sound filled the air of the slaughter-house as the bird silhouettes on the back wall began beating their wings frantically. The little black shapes struggled against the concrete as their tiny bodies fought the wall for freedom.

And a face emerged from high in the shadows, smiling the widest, most broken-toothed smile I'd ever seen.

6

All I could see in the shadows was a face as grey and pale as the moon, and that face was *wrong*. It was too big, for starters, too wide and too long by half. And it had only one eye. One good eye, anyway. The left one looked like it had been sewn up carelessly with black thread. But it was the smile that was really broken: it stretched across the too-big face, splitting it jaggedly in half. The smile was filled with too many teeth, two rows on top and two rows on bottom, and the teeth that weren't broken were razor sharp.

From somewhere deep in the shadows, a hand reached out. My brain told me the hand was too far away from the face to belong to the same creature, but it had to. Because the thing smiled wider still and gave me a little wave. It had too many joints in its long fingers, and they made a *click click click* sound when they bent.

I screamed.

For just three heartbeats, the birds in the wall stopped thrumming and the thing stopped smiling. Even I was surprised by the scream, but I also felt just a little better when it was out of me. I wanted to back away. To run.

But my hands refused to let go of the ladder. I was frozen.

"Oh, don't scream, little girl child. We aren't going to hurt her." The thing had a voice like shards of glass and wounded animals. It was layered, like there were many voices talking over one another, perfectly in sync. I was used to meeting unusual creatures in Blight Harbor, but this was the first one I'd encountered that I knew without a doubt could hurt me. More than that, I knew it *wanted* to.

I couldn't scream again if I tried. I could barely breathe. I thought a panic attack was running over me like a school bus, but then I realized it was just plain old terror. It was all I could do to stay standing. Without meaning to, I stepped behind the ladder, and then backward until my bare shoulders were against the bird-covered wall. I could feel them vibrating where my skin touched the concrete.

The thing kept talking and smiling, drawing closer toward my side of the wall. "Oh, pretty girl child with the pretty wheat-penny hair. We wouldn't hurt her yet. We will call her Pretty Penny, and she will call us The Clackity. We will talk and make a good, fair deal."

I was literally backed into a wall, and the thing—The Clackity?—was scuttling closer and closer. It dragged its shadows with it so even as it got near, all I could see was its face and that one long hand.

It drew nearer still. Close enough for me to look into its weepy yellow eye and see that the creature was totally and completely demented. The Clackity reached its clawed, extra-jointed hand out to touch me, and I thought it was going to put its hand in my hair like Aunt Desdemona liked to. In that moment, it was the very worst thing I could imagine.

I pressed against the wall hard, my body trying to push through it to safety. The Clackity's fingers were half an inch away, and I thought maybe I would start screaming again and never stop, when something burned my shoulder. The pain was white-hot and then gone in a flash, and I gasped in surprise and with the hurt of it. Though I didn't know what had caused it, I focused on the hurt and it helped. Just a little, but it helped.

The Clackity's face changed, and it pulled away from me with a look of something like disgust.

I glanced over my shoulder to see that one of the sparrows from the wall was no longer there. Instead it sat on my upper back, just above my right shoulder. I touched it softly. It was warm and a tiny bit raised, like I imagined a new tattoo would be.

It looked like this:

At least it did at first.

I remembered what Des had said about sparrows being protectors, and right then I'd take all the protection I could get. Even if it came in the shape of a bird tattoo.

The Clackity hissed at me, like I'd done something wrong. "Pretty Penny has an ugly birdie stain. Never mind. Never mind. The Clackity and the girl child can still make a fair, good deal. She can still be The Clackity's lucky penny."

As things became more unusual, somehow I got braver. I honestly think I was so scared that my brain couldn't process the fear anymore, so it just gave up trying. I reached down deep to find my warrior voice. All that came out was a squeak. "Where is my aunt? I'm going to go get her and bring her home."

The Clackity's one good eye widened, and then it began to laugh. The sound was metal shavings in a meat grinder. "Oh. Pretty Penny must go find her auntie before *he* does. That is part of our fair, good deal."

"Find her before who does?"

"The Cow and Piggy Man, of course."

When it said the name, the bird on my shoulder grew red-hot, like a warning.

"Who is the Cow and Piggy Man?" I asked. I was on confusion overload.

"Oh, she knows that man." The Clackity gave me a wink that said we shared a secret. "The bad, bad man who worked here long years ago. He did bad things, and if you could find all the fingers and toes, you could count them and know how many."

My mind buzzed. *The abattoir. Fingers and toes. Bad, bad man . . .*

And then I was sure I knew.

"Do you mean John Jeffrey Pope? But he disappeared, like, a hundred years ago."

The Clackity giggled. It was horrible, worse than its laugh. "Not disappeared, Penny. Long time dead. But bad, bad men make bad, bad ghosties. If her auntie is there"— it tapped the bird wall, pointing to whatever was beyond it—"and the Cow and Piggy Man is there, Pretty Penny had best find her first."

"How do I find her?" My best person was in there somewhere, and she might not know the ghost of John Jeffrey Pope was there too. I was going to go get her. I had to.

"Aaahhh. And here is our good, fair deal." Its smile got bigger and wider and there was nothing in that leer that made me want to smile back. "The Clackity will tell where her auntie is if she brings the Cow and Piggy Man back to us."

"How do I bring him back?"

"Easy, easy, Pretty Penny. She doesn't let him catch her. He will follow her back, but once he has her in the field, she'd better run and run and run." Clackity talked in riddles, but it meant *me*. It meant *I* had better run and run. "He'll follow her, and her auntie, too. But Pretty Penny is safe and sound in houses, safe until the field. And best before the sun goes down."

I had no idea whether I understood The Clackity, much less trusted it. But I knew I needed to get moving, find Desdemona, and bring her home.

Without her, I didn't *have* a home.

"Fine. Where is she?"

The shadow bird on my shoulder flapped its wings once. It felt like it was telling me, *Be careful.*

The Clackity smiled its biggest, most terrible smile. "First we will shake on our fair, good deal."

My whole body tensed and broke out in a cold sweat and said, *No. Absolutely not.* The very last thing I wanted to do was touch the creature swimming in shadows and talking in riddles, but I didn't see that I had much of a choice.

Des needed me.

I stuck my gross, sweaty hand out, waiting for The Clackity to grab it with its clicking fingers. As I did, the sparrow on my back flew up my shoulder, down my arm, and landed in the palm of my hand. All without ever leaving my skin. I could feel a gentle brush of feathers as it traveled across my body.

The Clackity watched the bird and quickly drew its own hand away.

It sneered at me. "Nasty birdie is making our Penny dreadful."

That was interesting. Some amazing part of my brain that was still working registered that The Clackity didn't like the bird. That still-functioning part of my brain also recognized that was something worth knowing.

The bird flapped its wings as it returned to my back. It was as anxious to get away from the mad creature as I was.

"Where is she?" I asked again.

The Clackity lowered its face until it was inches from mine. Its breath reeked of the abattoir, and of something else older and damp and rotten. "Seven houses," it whispered. "She has to go visit seven houses. Auntie will be waiting in the last one. One house at a time, one by one. No cheating, Pretty Penny. The houses won't let her. She gets to her auntie before the Cow and Piggy Man does and brings his ghostie to The Clackity. Then Pretty Penny and Auntie can go home to their sunshine life."

I couldn't blink, and I couldn't stop the words from coming out of my mouth. "And what if I don't bring him to you? What if I get my aunt and don't bring John Jeffrey Pope's ghost to you?"

"I'll eat the pretty girl child and I'll eat her pretty auntie. Gobble them up like treats, and we love treats because we are *always* so hungry." The Clackity smacked its lips together in anticipation, and I wondered how it managed to keep from cutting them on all those teeth.

My heart was racing so fast all the beats were running together. I studied the monster for a long, terrified moment. I didn't know if it could eat us, but I believed it would if it could. And I believed it would try.

If I wanted to get out of this alive, the smartest thing I could do right now was agree to whatever The Clackity told me to do. I'd figure out if I was telling it the truth later—when I was away from its awful smile. When I was far, far away from the suffocating smells of the abattoir made worse by that terrible creature. When I could breathe again. "Okay. I'll get Des from the seventh house. I'll save her, and I'll bring Pope back to you. Now, how do I go in? And how do I get out?"

The Clackity pointed to the stun shaft on the wall above us. "She gets out the same way her auntie went. The same way the cows and piggies came in."

I stared at the Clackity creature, trying to read the truth in its eye. "We have a deal, right? A good, fair deal?"

Clackity nodded. It was trying to make its face look solemn, but it wasn't working. "Indeed, Pretty Penny. We have a fair, good deal."

It was the closest I was going to get to a promise from the creature.

I climbed up the ladder as quickly as I dared, and more than once, my wet hands slipped on the rungs. All the while I kept an eye on The Clackity as it shifted and gibbered in the shadows. Somehow, I knew the little bird, newly and inexplicably tattooed on my back, was watching the creature too. And its whole tiny self felt puffed up—like it was doing its best to be intimidating. Like it was protecting me. That was simultaneously strange and reassuring.

As I made my way up the ladder, I realized no one but Des knew I'd been here at all. I was completely and totally on my own. The idea filled my legs with lead and made a hot, jagged little stone lodge in my throat. That stone grew and grew as I climbed and climbed until it almost cut off my breathing. *Almost but not quite.*

I pulled in a quick, shuddering breath as I hiked myself up into the steel tunnel of the stun shaft, trying hard not to think about what happened to all the animals that had passed through it so long before. Trying hard not to think about the thing that stood in the shadows below me.

As I steadied myself, a sound rushed up behind me and then surrounded me. A flock of sparrow silhouettes swarmed all around. They'd somehow pulled themselves from the wall to join me—us. My tattoo bird beat its shadow wings, happy to see its friends.

It was strange, the flock of shadow sparrows, but it wasn't scary. In fact, it was maybe the first non-scary thing to happen all day. Aunt Des had said they were good, and The Clackity didn't like them, and that meant I was glad to have them with me. I hoped they would stick around for a while.

Even though my legs didn't want to, I staggered through the metal stun shaft toward the wooden ramp that connected the abattoir with whatever was beyond. It was only a few steps, but in the short journey the light coming from the other side of the shaft darkened. I could hear The Clackity reminding me about our good, fair deal, but I was more focused on what was happening outside the shaft.

By the time I was clear of the stun shaft and at the top of the ramp, I realized I'd left Blight Harbor behind as well. The sky was my first clue—it had changed completely. Gone was the bright blue June day. It had been replaced by an infected purple color.

And the sun.

Somehow the sun was black, but it still managed to cast a strange light over the world below it. Wherever this was still had things like sky and sun, but they were *wrong*. Part of me wanted to turn and run back to the shaft, even if it meant having to face Clackity again. But that was just a little bit of me. Another part was set on exploring this place. But honestly, most of me just wanted to save my aunt.

I walked down the long wooden ramp, which ended abruptly in the field. It was cooler there than it had been in the abattoir, cooler than it had been anywhere in Blight Harbor for the last week. And the air smelled different too. Out here, it had almost an . . . underground quality. It had the damp, dirt smell of a cave. Or a grave. I pushed that last thought away.

The grass in the field was as black as the sun. Beyond the field, I saw the familiar glow of neighborhood lights. Between me and them, at the far edge of the field, stood a gate. At least I knew where I was going. That thought made me laugh out loud, startling the shadow birds. It was ironic to think I knew where I was going when I didn't even know where I was.

I felt a little like Dorothy on the yellow brick road, except instead of a golden path, I had a wide field of scratchy black grass and a gate.

"I hope there are seven houses out there," I said to the sparrows.

I hiked up my backpack and started walking.

7

The grass in the field wasn't grass at all. At least, not any grass I'd ever seen before. There was no wind, not even a breeze, but the long dark blades shifted and swayed anyway. If I stood in one place too long, they clung to my legs, asking me to stay for a while. And they weren't exactly black, but a green so dark it was easy to mistake for black. When I picked a blade to inspect it, an emerald-green goo oozed out that smelled like a cross between gasoline and old perfume. I didn't like to think what would happen if a thunderstorm rolled in and lightning hit the field.

I moved a little faster.

Behind me, the back of the abattoir stood as I'd left it. Now it didn't look defiant. It looked *ready*. And I liked that a whole lot less than defiant.

The flock of silhouette sparrows began to flutter erratically, darting around but keeping close to me. They seemed nervous, and that made *me* nervous. The sparrow on my shoulder burned and itched like a blistering sunburn, which felt like a warning, which *also* made me nervous. There was a sensation on the back of my neck that made me think of animals in the wild, the feeling that says, *Careful, someone is watching you.* The Clackity was probably keeping an eye on me. But there was also John Jeffrey Pope to worry about, somewhere in this world. The Clackity said I would be safe until I came back from the houses and through the field. Still, I wanted to get out of that wide-open field, where there was nowhere to hide.

I stood as tall and strong as I could, even though I felt small and helpless. I focused on the gate in the distance and on my new bird tattoo. I didn't run, because running would be admitting I was scared, and that would be like inviting a panic attack, but I did walk a whole lot faster than usual. In my mind I could hear Aunt Desdemona saying, *If you don't strut, how's anyone supposed to know you own the place?* And that made me smile a little and want to cry all at the same time. I looked like a warrior, but I needed to act like one too. For Aunt Des, if not for me. I wasn't about to let Pope or anything else think I was going to be an easy target.

The field was maybe twice the size of a football field, big enough to take a few minutes to walk, but not big enough to lose sight of the slaughterhouse from the other side. I headed toward the gate at the far north side of the field. Beyond it I could make out the vague outlines and lights of a neighborhood. A neighborhood told me someone—or something—lived there. I wasn't sure if that idea made me feel better or worse.

When I reached the gate, it seemed taller than it had appeared from the field. No, I decided, it really *was* taller now than it had been—at first it had looked like a normal

ten-foot gate. Up close I could see it was much, *much* taller.
I was bad at estimating things like height, but I figured it
had to reach up at least thirty feet. Maybe more. And it
was as wide as it was tall. The gate was made of blackened wrought iron, all twisted metal and sharp spires,
and was older than anything I'd ever seen before. Usually
gates have fences, too. But not this one. If there had been
a fence once, it had rotted away. Or been torn down.

There was something hanging from the latch on the
right side. As I drew closer, I recognized it. I should—I'd
seen it every day since I'd moved to Blight Harbor. It
was Aunt Desdemona's small black purse. She carried it
everywhere, even when she moved from room to room
in our house.

I'd teased her about the purse once. She'd answered
me in a way that suggested she was kidding but also very
serious, saying that she would be ready for the zombie
apocalypse at any time. *Stick with me, kiddo,* she'd told
me, holding up the little bag. *I can get us out of almost
anything Blight Harbor throws at us.*

And now the purse was here, instead of with Aunt
Des. Seeing it hanging on the gate like that, I had to
believe she'd left it for me to find. I didn't like thinking
that she had given it up, because in a way, that felt like
she had given up. And I kind of wanted to give up too,
even though I'd barely gotten started.

All of a sudden, it was too much.

If I was scared of an open field, and if a purse made
me want to collapse and cry like a little kid, how was I
possibly going to get through whatever was coming? I

wasn't a warrior. I was just a girl who couldn't control her own fear, whose panic jerked her around like marionette strings, who couldn't even remember how to breathe sometimes. I'd always needed Des to make sure I was okay. She was the strong one.

There was no way I could do this without her, much less save her.

The flock of shadow sparrows hovered in midair like they were waiting for me to make up my mind. It didn't help.

I almost sat down against the gate at the edge of the field, almost gave up right then to wait for whatever was eventually going to come and get me. And if nothing came to get me, I'd just sit there forever until the black grass grew up all around me and I disappeared and . . .

And then I felt something light flutter over my shoulder and nuzzle my collarbone. Something that shouldn't be able to nuzzle because it was just a shadow. The little bird tattoo.

A small voice in my head said, *One more step. Then another. And then another after that. That's all. That's all you have to do for now.* And that voice in my head was *mine*, sort of, but it belonged to something else, too. I reached up and touched the little bird—*my* little bird— and it ruffled its feathers under my fingertips. As strange as it was, the little bird felt *right*. If anything, it was the only right thing in this whole wrong place. I needed someone to help tell me what to do, and if that someone was an impossible bird tattoo, well, that was going to have to work.

I made myself breathe until I could take deep, regular breaths. Then I took D's purse down from the gate to zip it away in my backpack. I peeked into it first to see if there was anything helpful inside, like a clue or a note or something.

There wasn't.

Leaning forward, I put my hands on the bars of the gate and poked my face through them to get a better look at the houses beyond. The metal was too warm, like it had been soaking up the heat of that black sun since the beginning of time, and greasy. I wiped my hands on my jeans, but there was nothing on them but drying sweat.

I couldn't get a good look at the houses—there was a thick haze between me and them. Not a fog, because it was clear. It was like trying to see something through translucent, moving water.

On either side of the gate there was absolutely nothing. No fence, no wall, no barrier of any kind. The bars looked heavy and hard to open, so I decided to walk around the gate instead. As I moved toward the open space to the left of the gate, the sparrow flock grew agitated. By the time I reached the very end of the gate, they were pecking at me.

"Ow, knock it off! I get it, I'll go through. I didn't even know you guys *could* peck." I swatted at the flying silhouettes as I turned around and went back to the center of the opening. I wasn't sure what the shadow birds knew, but I figured that since they seemed to be on my side, I'd trust them.

As predicted, the latch was hard to slide. When it finally moved, it did so with a *skree* of protest that filled the quiet day. The sound announced our arrival, not that I had been trying to sneak in. The gate *was* heavy, and I leaned my whole body into it to force it open. It took work, but I finally made a space big enough for me and my backpack to squeeze through.

Once in, I looked back at the little swarm of black birds. They didn't follow me beyond the gate.

"Hey, little guys, aren't you coming with me?"

In answer, they all stopped fluttering and hovered midair. They weren't coming in. But when I looked to my shoulder, I noticed my little buddy was still there.

"How about you, Bird? You staying with me?"

He—for some reason I was sure Bird was a *he*—flew a tight little circle around my back and returned to his perch on my shoulder, where he folded up his tattoo wings. He was settling in.

I was relieved. I wasn't going into this entirely alone.

"Okay, little friends. Wait for me? I'll be back as soon as I can with Aunt Des. Then we'll get her out of here. You guys can come home with us if you want."

The little black birds just hung in the air. They bobbed up and down in breezes so small I couldn't feel them. I sighed and waved goodbye, which felt both silly and appropriate.

I turned back to face the neighborhood, and to decide what to do next. The air between me and the houses was still hazy and thick. It extended on either side as far as I could see. I didn't see any option but to walk through it. So I did.

It took only a few steps to get through the mist and to the other side, maybe ten seconds. A horrible ten seconds. That mist was magic, but it was a bad sort of magic. As soon as I walked into the haze, my head filled with every terrible thing that had ever happened to me, from little moments to the giant, awful events that had changed my life. And every bad thing I'd ever said or done rushed over me like a dark flood.

Kids laughing at me for falling off my bike.

Being teased for my red hair.

Accidentally knocking over and breaking the glass Christmas angel when I was four, and then lying about it.

The fire.

Mom and Dad missing.

A funeral with no bodies.

And . . .

And then I broke through and was on the other side. I didn't step out of the haze—I stumbled out and fell to my knees. I was filled up with all the worst fear and pain and guilt I'd ever felt. My stomach churned and I almost threw up. Head down, almost touching the ground, I forced myself to take big, even breaths until my heart slowed down and my trembling stopped. Bird stroked my back with his wings.

That mist, whatever it was, was made up of all the real-life nightmares I'd ever had. If leaving this place meant going through that again, I wasn't sure I'd be able to do it. But there would be time to worry about that later. After the houses.

Still on my knees, I lifted my head and got my first good look at the houses that made up the strange little neighborhood in this strange little world. I don't know what I expected, but this wasn't it.

PART TWO

Safe as Houses

8

As The Clackity had promised, there were seven houses.

They were arranged in a half circle, all with their front doors facing me. I couldn't see a road or even a path leading to them. I was honestly a little confused, because after meeting The Clackity, I figured any place it would send me to would be terrifying. This . . . wasn't. I mean, the houses didn't make any sense together, and it was weird for sure, but it wasn't scary. I started to feel a little more confident.

Maybe this wouldn't be so bad after all.

The house on the far left was large and white, a farm-house without a farm. Its paint was yellowing in places. It looked like any farmhouse anywhere, and there was nothing special about it.

The next house was hideous and black, every inch decorated and ornate. It was the biggest house in the neighborhood by a long shot. That house was something a whole lot worse than haunted. I knew in my heart it was dangerous.

Then came a small wooden house—a cabin, really, that belonged somewhere deep in the forest.

Right in the middle was a modern-looking, ocean-blue house with lots of glass. It looked like it should be on the cover of a magazine.

Then came a simple, square, beige house. It was as plain as a house could be. There were potted flowers and a small porch, but those were totally ordinary too.

The next one was made entirely of candy. Like real, sugary candy. Everyone knows a candy house is a trick, or a trap, so I'd have to be really careful with that one.

Finally my gaze fell on the house on the far right. It was beautiful, light yellow with white trim, made up of two stories and a covered front porch with a rocking chair. It was a perfect house for a child to grow up in. My head hurt looking at it, and at first I wasn't sure why. It took my brain a couple of seconds to sort it out and when it did, my heart hurt too.

Somehow, my childhood home was standing at the edge of a field behind an abattoir. If any of the houses scared me, I guess it was that one, because it should have been nothing but ash in the dirt a thousand miles away. And because it meant The Clackity knew way more about me than I could have suspected.

I wasn't ready to go to my yellow house. I wasn't ready to face whatever I was going to find there. And if I was being totally honest, a tiny little part of me that was still eight years old hoped with her whole entire self that my parents would be in there waiting for me. I *knew* they wouldn't be, but knowing didn't keep that little part from believing. I'd learned a long time ago that hope hurt more than almost anything else. I wanted to yell at that little part of me, to tell her she was being stupid and that daydreaming only made things worse. But I couldn't: it wasn't her fault, and she didn't know any better. For a long time—the worst time—hope was all she had.

So, yeah, I wasn't ready to go to my house right then. Besides, I knew in my gut Desdemona wouldn't be in my yellow house. I was pretty sure it was the first house I was supposed to enter, not the last, and Clackity said Des would be in the last house.

Just to be sure—and I guess because I was stalling, too—I sprinted to the white farmhouse and tried the front door. It was locked. As I twisted the knob, my little sparrow buddy surprised me by pecking my shoulder seven times, fast and mean.

"Ow!" I growled and slapped at my shoulder. "Knock it off, Bird. I get it. This is the seventh house." I tried peering in the windows, but heavy toile curtains covered them all. Instead of the usual pattern of children playing or animals on farms, the fabric was made up of screaming skeletons where the people should have been.

It looked like this:

As I inspected the window frames and the siding on the house, I realized something I'd missed at first— something unsettling, and scary, too. The paint wasn't yellowing. There *was* no paint. The whole house was made out of bones. Bones of all sizes. And some of those were yellow with age. I worked hard not to think too much about where, or who, those bones had come from.

I ran out to where the front yard should have been, cupped my hands around my mouth, and yelled, "Aunt Des! Desdemona! Hold on! I won't leave you! I'm coming for you! Just . . . hold on." It was silly. There should have been something else I could say. A way to make her believe I would, I *could*, rescue her. But the words wouldn't come. "Love you," I whispered.

I watched the windows for a sign that she was in the bone house. There was nothing.

I knew what I had to do next. I had to get started. Seven houses, one at a time.

And the first house was my house.

It hit me suddenly, hard enough to make me catch my breath—I wanted with all my heart to go in, to see it again. And I was so scared of what I would find. I ignored that bright, hot little eight-year-old part of me, deep in my stomach, that thought, *Maybe.* Just maybe, Mom and Dad would be in there waiting.

The sparrow on my shoulder pecked me gently. *Get moving.*

Something like gravity was doing its best to keep my feet planted, and I wasn't sure I was strong enough to take the next step or the one after that.

I sighed. "Yeah, buddy. I know."

I walked toward my house, slowly at first, and then began to jog. As I passed the gate I'd come through only a few minutes before, I got that neck-prickly feeling again and spun around in a half circle. Through the haze, I could see the shape of a man dressed in dark clothes behind the iron bars. He stood on the other side of the gate, not moving.

The Cow and Piggy Man.

John Jeffrey Pope.

He lifted one hand in a lazy wave.

I didn't wave back.

I ran.

I ran up the steps to my house, avoiding the middle of the third step with the loose board Dad never got around to fixing. The big wooden chair Mom had made while on one of her arts-and-crafts kicks sat on the porch to the left of the front door, just like it was supposed to. An American flag hung from the front corner post. It waved gently, even though the air didn't move.

Everything was perfect.

Maybe . . . That awful, hopeful little voice refused to stay quiet.

At least, everything *seemed* perfect until I stopped to catch my breath and turned to look at the scene beyond my porch. A plum sky, a giant iron gate, a black sun. Way out in the almost-black grass, a slaughterhouse with The Clackity inside. And, somewhere in that field, the ghost of a serial killer.

This was *not* my neighborhood. This was *not* my house.

Remember, I told myself. *Remember why you're here.*

I grasped the brass doorknob and turned it, eager to get moving. It didn't budge.

I stared at the doorknob in my hand and tried it again. Slower this time. Then I turned it the other way. Then I jiggled it.

The door was locked.

How could it be locked? This was the first house. It *had* to be the first house.

I sat down hard on the porch steps and put my head in my hands. I nudged at the loose board on the step with my toe as I thought. I worried the board, and my mind drifted. *Dad never would get around to fixing the step. It made Mom crazy. And there was that time Mom locked herself out of the house. She got so mad. Said we'd put the board to good use. After that . . .*

After that day, we never got locked out of the house again. Because Mom hid a spare key under the board.

I held my breath as I leaned down and pried up the wiggly piece of wood so a corner stuck up and I could just get my hand underneath. I ran my fingers carefully on the underside of the board until they touched the edge of the duct tape I knew—hoped—would be there. I worked the edge of the tape gingerly. If the key fell off the tape and deeper into the stairs, this would all get a lot more complicated.

It didn't.

I grasped the end of the key and pulled gently, feeling the tape pop and peel away from the metal. When the brass key was free, I brought it slowly out from under the board. It glinted dark gold in the black sun.

Sitting there on the porch steps, the key to my old life in my hand, I started to cry. I cried because of a little girl's refusal to stop believing, and I cried because I knew better. I cried hard, but not for very long. When I was done, I wiped tears and snot off my face with the back of my hand. A smudge of black eyeliner came off too.

I held the key tight, letting it bite into my palm. It was the key I had to focus on. And the houses. And Aunt Des. There would be plenty of time to feel sad when all this was over.

"Thanks, Mom. Thanks, Dad." I said it out into the air, even though I prayed they weren't anywhere near this messed-up place. With every part of me, I hoped they couldn't see me, or hear me, right then. So, I guess I did still have hope after all. It was just a different kind.

When I tried the key in the door, it worked. Just like I knew it would.

I closed my eyes, pushed the door open, and stepped into the house that wasn't my house.

Everything was right. All the furniture and books and knickknacks were where they were supposed to be. Even the plants, lined up on the deep windowsill in our dining room, were green and healthy. It even smelled right, that smell that only your home has and you don't even know it's there until you've been away for a long, long time. In my yellow house, that smell was citrus candles and coffee and sunlight warm through the front-room curtains.

I rounded the corner from our dining room to the short hallway that led to my bedroom.

Hanging in the hall were a bunch of family pictures, all in black frames, just like there should have been. I never thought I would see them again, but there they were. The pictures were frozen in time—because they were pictures, but also because they stopped when I was eight. Because that was when the fire happened and that's when our family stopped too.

My favorite was where it was supposed to be. A photo of just my mom, which meant my dad had been behind the camera. She was sitting on a red blanket in the grass, smiling big from behind her signature violet, tortoise-shell glasses. She had one hand held palm out like she was telling my dad, *Stop! Don't take my picture!*

I pressed my own hand up against photo-Mom's hand. When I was little, we did that all the time to see whose hand was bigger. She always won. I wondered if she would win now, or if my hand had grown as big as hers. More tears came and I just let them fall. I missed my mom and I missed my dad. Time made the missing different, but it didn't make it go away.

I pulled my hand from the glass, wiped at my eyes, and made my way to my bedroom.

It was a little girl's pink-and-purple nightmare of a room. I had loved it. My blankets and little rug and unicorn collection were all exactly as they should have been. I didn't touch anything. I guess I was kind of afraid that as soon as I did it would all disappear, like in a dream. And I wasn't quite ready for it to be gone again. Not yet.

Then I noticed my room was neater than I had ever kept it.

In fact, the whole house was neater than it had ever been.

I took another walk through each room on the first floor, really looking at everything this time.

My parents had always been busy with work and with me. My mom had school at night too. The house was never perfect. There were always books and papers in the dining room, keys and gloves in the kitchen. Blankets and pillows in the living room were tossed on the couch to be straightened later, and my bedroom was always one puzzle or game away from being a complete disaster. I considered going upstairs to my parents' bedroom, but the thought of seeing their bed neatly made and laundry put away instead of in a pile waiting to be folded made my eyes sting with fresh tears. I wanted to keep the memory of their room as it really had been—cozy and a little messy and smelling like my mom's perfume.

This house was all so right that it was wrong. And that made things better—easier—because I could tell the little girl with all her daydreams that she could go back to sleep for now. This was decidedly not my house.

Then I noticed the picture in the living room on the mantel above the fireplace. It was supposed to be an oversized print of a photo from my parents' wedding. Only now, it was turned around so the back of the frame faced the room.

I was afraid. Something about that backward photograph made me scared all the way into my ribs and my lungs. My breathing was fast and not very deep, and my hands were cold as I reached up and turned the picture to face the room.

My parents were gone. Instead my aunt Desdemona

sat on a small wooden table wearing her prettiest black summer dress. She looked over her shoulder with big, nervous eyes. A man stood behind her. His smile was wide and handsome. Sandy hair fell over one eye. Pope looked directly at me from the photograph. His hand rested on my aunt's shoulder like it belonged there.

It didn't. It didn't belong there at all.

I wanted to scream at him to stop touching her, to give my aunt back.

And I might have screamed, but the sound of creaking boards distracted me. Someone was on the front porch.

I pushed back the curtains hanging in the tall, narrow window by the front door and found myself looking at the real John Jeffrey Pope. Or his ghost, anyway. He looked almost alive except when the sun caught him just right and shone through his edges. I had stood just as close to a lot of ghosts—closer even—but never one that felt as awful as Pope. He was so full of evil, he radiated the stuff like a stench. I froze, hoping (but not really believing) I wouldn't be seen.

Pope was leaning down, shielding his eyes from the glare of the black sun to get a better look inside not-my-house. When he saw me, his lips twitched up in amusement and he gave me a little wave with the hand not shielding his eyes. Then he reached down to the doorknob.

It shifted under his hand, but it didn't turn. A look of confusion crossed his face. He tried again, jiggling the handle, same as I had. I could see the door wasn't locked. He just couldn't open it.

I was too afraid to scream. Too afraid to move. But I

was not so afraid that I forgot what The Clackity had told me in the abattoir: *Safe and sound in houses, safe until the field. And best before the sun goes down.*

Pope gave the handle one last, violent rattle. The whole door shook in its frame. When nothing happened and it didn't budge, he put his hands in his pockets and stared at it for a while. Then he leaned toward the window, studying me like a thing in a cage, and mouthed, "Bye, Evelyn. See you soon."

He didn't smile.

I didn't like it when he smiled, but the not smiling was maybe worse. Because he wasn't pretending to be my friend anymore. He wasn't pretending he wouldn't hurt me. Or Des. And he was scary—scarier than The Clackity by a mile. Because in his eyes I didn't see anything but meanness and determination.

My knees were about as solid as water and my heart was high up in my throat, but I did my best to look calm because I didn't want him to see I wasn't. Sometimes we are who other people think we are, and I needed John Jeffrey Pope to believe I was brave.

I watched as, hands in his pockets, he strolled down the steps and away from the house. Faintly, I could hear him whistling.

I turned back to face the living room.

Everything had changed.

A coat of dust covered every surface in the room, and more was falling from an invisible source in the ceiling. I rubbed a shiny brown streak across the coffee table and smelled the dust on my fingers.

Not dust. Ash.

Of course it was ash.

And then the air was so filled with the smell of smoke it was hard to breathe. I couldn't actually *see* smoke anywhere, just the snowing powder, but the smell was all around me.

The first house was a ghost of my house, and it was going to burn in the ghost of the fire that had destroyed mine. I didn't want to watch it happen, wasn't sure I could handle it. I'd seen the ashes the first time, after the real fire, when I insisted I was being lied to, that my house hadn't burned to the ground. Des had brought me herself, knowing I needed to see it was true. Which meant she'd been with me for my first panic attack. Reliving that moment seemed like a terrible idea, then or ever.

I had to get to the second house, but first, I needed to figure out why I was here in this one. What did I need to do before I went to the second house? It had to be something—Clackity wouldn't have sent me on a tour down memory lane for no reason.

Get the next key, dummy. The voice in my head was my own, but my little sparrow buddy was beating against my shoulders with his tiny wings. The voice was mine, but I wasn't so sure the words were.

The next house in the row was the candy house. I'd read enough books to know there were a million reasons not to go into a candy house, but I didn't think I had much choice. And anything would be better than the suffocating air in this house that was not-my-house.

I tore from room to room, looking for a key that

would fit a house made of sugar. The ash piled up and the rooms began to darken around the corners. The walls were burning from the inside. I didn't have long.

Back in not-my-bedroom, I dug through drawers and jewelry boxes. There was no key, just a little girl's trinkets and treasures. On not-my-bed, stuffed animals and dolls were almost completely covered with flakes of ash. I could still see a few of their faces, and each of their left eyes had been stitched closed with thick black thread, just like the creature in the abattoir. If it was The Clackity's idea of a joke, it wasn't a very good one. I wasn't crying anymore. And for a minute I wasn't scared.

I was mad.

I grabbed a handful of stuffed things and threw them across the room with a scream of frustration. They fell apart before they hit the wall, becoming more ash in the air.

With nothing to be found in the bedroom, I went back to the hallway. I put my hand on Mom's one last time. And it really was the last time, because the photo crumbled under my touch, just more cinders now. My heart broke all over again and I wanted to scoop up the ashes of the photo and put them in my pocket, but there was no time and they were all mixed up with the ash from everything else. I reminded myself Mom wasn't really there, and this wasn't really my house. It was then I noticed that the little part in me had stopped hoping, and it turned out not hoping could hurt too, in an empty and endless sort of way.

I ran into the kitchen for the first time. There, on the

counter, was a shiny red-and-white bowl I had never seen before. Mom would never have used it. It wasn't her style. Ash floated around the bowl, but didn't land on it, almost like it wasn't allowed. The bowl was as big as a cooking pot and gleamed bright in the grey light of the room.

The bowl was full of round hard candies. They shone like little sugar gems. I dug through them until my sweaty fingers got sticky. I began to scoop out the candy, scattering it across the slowly burning kitchen. At the bottom of the bowl was duct-taped an enamel key. It was striped a dozen different colors, like the fruit-flavored candy canes I loved. A red ribbon was tied around the end of the key. On the ribbon, in pretty, swirly letters, was written *Hurry*.

So I did.

I slipped the key into my jeans pocket. It clinked against the brass key that opened the yellow house. Fast now, I walked through the kitchen toward the mudroom, which doubled as a laundry room. At the back door of not-my-house, I took one last look around. The walls were almost entirely black, and the ceilings were beginning to sag. There was still no visible smoke, and no heat, but the house was burning down just the same.

This was no accident.

This was no coincidence.

My house—my *real* house—had burned when I was eight. I wasn't there when it happened, but my parents were. Or they were supposed to be. After the fire, no one could find them, alive or otherwise. So I was sent to live with Aunt Des.

No, the not-my-house first house was some kind of

test. The Clackity wanted to see if I was tough enough to make it through this long, scary day. Or maybe it wanted to see if it could make me quit.

I wouldn't.

I went out the back door and closed it behind me, just like Mom always told me to. The idea brought fresh tears to my eyes, but I swallowed them back. I was extra slow and quiet as I stepped outside. I had no idea where Pope had gone, if he was waiting for me around a corner or behind a fence. Freaking out wouldn't do me any good, but I had to be careful. And on the lookout.

The air outside was clean and bright by comparison. After the invisible smoke in not-my-house, I could taste the hints of whatever grew in the fields. It flavored the air with roses and gasoline.

I walked into the backyard. The grass was shorter here, like it got mowed on Saturdays, but it was the same almost-black as the field. I stood in the middle of not-my-backyard and watched as the house that wasn't my house burned down in an invisible fire. It happened fast, and in a matter of minutes nothing but ash floated where the copy of my beautiful yellow home had been.

10

From the giant gate, the houses had looked as close to one another as the houses in a regular neighborhood. Because they were. I *knew* they were because I had walked from the seventh house to the first in just a few minutes. And that would have *stayed* true in a world where there were rules and logic.

But standing behind the remains of the burned yellow house, I couldn't even *see* the next one. A thick forest now grew between them. A narrow dirt-and-stone path started at the edge of the yard I stood in and disappeared into the dark woods. Somewhere, at the end of that path, was a candy house.

"This is stupid," I said, trying to convince myself it was true. I had always been a city kid—or at least a small-town kid—and didn't know much about the forest (aside from my Lily Lessons, of course). What I *did* know were fairy tales, and that was enough for me to know that nothing good came of walking down a path in the woods that had appeared out of nowhere. *Especially* when that path led to a candy house.

My buddy beat his wings twice, giving me a little pat

on the back. *It's all right. Get going before you lose your nerve.*

"I'm going, I'm going." And I was. I didn't like being out in the open—it was too close to being out in the field, exposed. "Just tell me if there's anything behind me, okay?"

I took the fluttering of Bird's wings as agreement.

My backpack was heavier than it had been before, or maybe it was just all the weight I felt on my shoulders. Either way, I hitched it up and started into the woods.

I was only a few steps in when I heard shifting and rustling behind me. I spun around to find myself faced not with the burned remnants of not-my-house, but with more forest. The woods hadn't just closed in behind me; they had taken over everything as far as I could see in any direction. I was a little creeped out by the moving trees, but I was also relieved. I wouldn't be tempted to keep looking back over my shoulder for something that wasn't really there—my old house and my old life. For the time being, I'd be able to leave the past in the past where it belonged, and not obsess over what-ifs and maybes.

As best I knew, forests were supposed to be made up of trees that were all pretty much alike. Here, the trees weren't even close to uniform. Some were tall and spindly; others were short and thick. Some looked like pines, others like maples. But most of them looked like they had been drawn by someone who'd never seen a real tree before. Branches shot out crazily, sometimes sharp like needles and sometimes twisted like ropes. Several grew through or around each other, fighting for the same bit of space. What they *did* have in common was color. All the trunks were a shade of red, from blood to brick. And all the leaves were the same green-black as the field.

Staring straight up, I could find little patches of purple sky if I looked hard enough. I think I would have stayed there for a while, trying to make sense of the weird landscape, if a twig hadn't snapped in the woods off to my right.

At least that was what it sounded like. But then the sound was followed by a second snap, and then a third. And then more than I could count.

Out of the forest, and directly onto the path, stepped a small grey fawn. If it hadn't been standing right in front of me, it would have been easy to miss—its dappled fur blended in with all the shadows and bits of light poking through the forest. It sniffed at the ground and delicately pulled at something it found there.

I'd never been close to a deer before, and I approached it cautiously. I thought maybe, if I was calm and quiet, I could even stroke its soft-looking pelt.

My sparrow began to beat his wings. Softly at first, then frantically. "Knock it off, Bird," I whispered, and smacked at him.

The sound startled the little creature in front of me. It looked up in my direction for the first time. One black eye shone in the filtered forest light. The other was sewn up with black thread. As it tilted its head, I realized it hadn't been the sound of snapping twigs I'd heard. Every time the animal moved, it click-click-clicked like long, bony fingers with too many joints. As my brain tried to make sense of the creature in front of me, it also flashed back to the dolls in not-my-bedroom. All the stuffed things with sewn-up eyes.

"The Clackity." I was scared, but something else was swelling up inside me. I was angry, too. Clackity hadn't just been mean, sending me to not-my-house. It had been cruel. And nothing made me angrier than big people— or monsters—who were cruel to smaller, weaker ones. Clackity may not have been a person, but as far as I was concerned, the same rules applied. I was determined to prove to it I wasn't as small and weak as it seemed to think I was.

The fawn smiled a too-wide smile that was full of broken razor teeth. The shadow it cast was too big and too dark for such a small animal, and it slid around on its own, circling the hooves of the little creature like oily smoke.

"The Clackity," I repeated. I tried to sound brave and stern. "You never said you were going to spy on me. You never said you were going to try to scare me. That was *not* part of our fair, good deal."

It turned out deer could shrug. At least that one could.

I could feel Bird creeping up over my shoulder like he had in the abattoir. And it gave me an idea. I just hoped my buddy and I were on the same page.

I stepped closer to the Clackity fawn and reached out to pet it between the ears. Just as my hand rested on its fur, Bird flew into my palm.

The fawn let out a howl like a wild and injured

thing—which I guess it kind of was—and twisted away from me. Its shadow pulled back and I saw that it wasn't a shadow at all, but a thousand black spiders that clicked and clacked as they scattered into the forest.

When the fawn looked back up, it had two regular, clear eyes. In those eyes I saw something that looked a lot like gratitude, and I swear it dipped its head in a tiny bow before it ran off into the woods.

I'd managed to scare The Clackity off, but chances were good I'd made it angry, too. "Well, Bird. That was either the best idea I've ever had, or it was the worst."

Bird returned to my shoulder and fluffed his feathers.

"Yeah, I agree. It was pretty cool. Good work, by the way."

The sparrow on my skin puffed up just a bit, proud of himself.

This time, when I hitched my backpack up, I tried not to squish Bird too much.

I checked my pocket to make sure the keys were still there. Then we headed down the winding path in search of a candy house.

11

As Bird and I approached a sharp bend in the path, the trees started to change. They straightened up tall like proper trees and began to look like they all belonged to the same forest. And while their colors didn't change—they were still red and black—almost everything else about them did.

It started slowly, but by the time I realized what was happening, nearly all the trees we passed were made of licorice. Black and red twisted together to form trunks and branches and leaves. The scent filled the air, sharp and sweet. It was nice at first, a welcome break from the smell of the green-black grass, but soon I started to feel sick from it.

The path cut into a particularly thick grove of licorice trees. Heavy with their sticky leaves, branches drooped so low over the path I had to duck under them. When I came out the other side, I stepped into a clearing. It was large enough for square garden patches and raised flower beds, and in the center of the clearing, the candy house shimmered under the black sun and purple sky. Even from a distance, the wind carried the bright scent of all the things growing in the neat little garden.

It would have been straight out of a storybook if it hadn't been for the three people who crawled around on their hands and knees in the dark grass. They moved slowly, with their faces close to the ground, grass catching in their hair. From where I stood, I couldn't tell much about the trio, and I definitely couldn't tell whether they were friendly or dangerous. What was clear was that they were looking for something.

"Do you think we're supposed to help them?" I whispered to Bird.

Wings tapped my shoulder three times, firmly. It felt like, *Yes, but be careful.*

"Got it," I told him.

I made my way toward the crawling figures. I expected them to look up as soon as I began to move in their direction. None of them did. They continued on hands and knees to search for whatever it was they'd lost.

As I got closer, I could hear muttering, disgruntled voices. The three ladies—because it turned out that was what they were—argued with one another as they combed through the grass with their fingers. They were maybe Aunt D's age, not old exactly, but maybe too old to be crawling around on the lawn.

"Are you sure this is where you dropped it?" a golden-haired woman with a voice like wind chimes asked. She wore a dress the color of sunshine, and she sounded like a kind teacher growing tired of talking to a confused child.

"Yes. Of course I'm sure, twit." A voice filled with gravel came from a grey-haired woman. Bits of grass

were stuck in her grey sweater, and I imagined the knees of her matching pants were probably stained and ruined.

"I think I've found—oh. Never mind." The nervous, tittering voice belonged to a woman with pale pink hair and a flowery pink dress that wasn't really suited for hanging out in the yard.

I was so close I was nearly standing over them. Not one of the three had so much as glanced in my direction. The whole situation was getting uncomfortable.

Bird fluttered anxiously. *Do something already.*

So I did. Kind of. "Um. Excuse me?"

The golden woman answered me without looking up. "I'm sorry, darling. You'll have to come back another time. We're quite busy at the moment."

It was a strange way to answer someone who'd just shown up in your backyard. "I . . . well, I didn't actually say why I'm here."

"We don't care why you're here," snapped the grey lady. She didn't bother making eye contact, or even turning her head in my general direction.

"There's no reason to be nasty about it." The words came out before I could stop them.

The pink lady tried to placate us all while peering at the ground. "Why are you here then, dear?"

I wasn't really sure how to answer that. "It's complicated."

"No time for complicated!" The grey lady really was the worst.

I decided it was time to try a different approach. "Can I help you find whatever it is you're looking for?" Maybe if I helped them, they'd be willing to help me. I wasn't sure what I needed from them yet, but the three ladies didn't have sewn-up eyes and they weren't John Jeffrey Pope, so I figured they were the safest people I'd encountered all day.

"That would be lovely," said the golden lady.

"Yes, please. If it isn't too much trouble," said the pink lady.

"Harrumph," harrumphed the grey lady.

"What is it we're looking for, exactly?"

"The key, of course, twit," Grey barked.

"It's smallish and has parts that go in a lock," explained Pink, unhelpfully.

"And it is quite colorful and has a ribbon tied about the end," added Gold, more helpfully.

Right then I knew I *could* help them. I reached into my pocket and pulled out the candy-dish key. It certainly matched the description, right down to being smallish with parts that went in a lock. "You don't mean this key, do you?"

All three women turned at once to look in my direction.

In that moment I realized a number of things I hadn't known until right then.

Most importantly, I knew beyond a doubt that I was dealing with witches. That idea didn't scare me nearly as much as you might think it would.

The three women squinted up at me, struggling to see what I held in my hand. It wasn't their near blindness that convinced me they were witches (although I'd learned witches generally have terrible eyesight from years of dealing with noxious plants and various poisons).

I knew Pink, Gold, and Grey were witches because they all looked so much alike. Which meant all three of them also looked very much like Head Librarian Lily Littleknit, my second-best person and the only other witch I personally knew. It had never been a secret that Lily was a witch, but it took me a while to really understand it after I first moved to Blight Harbor. I think it hit home for me the time she sweetened my lemonade by tapping the glass with her finger. That was when I realized my friend could do honest-to-goodness magic and not just plant and herb stuff.

Grey reached out to snatch the key from my hand and missed by a mile. I slipped the key back into my pocket in case she tried again and got lucky.

Pink started crying.

Gold said in her musical voice, "We've been looking for that for some time now."

"How long?" I asked.

"Oh, a month. Give or take a few days." Gold smiled as best she could, but there were dark circles under her eyes. She looked so much like Lily, tired after a long day at the library, that it made me want to help her and cry all at the same time. "We would very much like to go inside our house, retrieve our glasses, and sit on something that isn't rocks and dirt."

The three witches stood, moving stiffly, Pink helping Grey up off the ground. As predicted, their knees were grass-stained darkest green from days of crawling about.

Like Lily, they all had wide eyes, pointed chins, and thick, arched eyebrows. And each had a dark mole—more beauty mark than wart—on the left side of her face. Also, like Lily, they were almost monochromatic, with hair and skin and eyes all just different shades of the same colors. Even Pink's light brown eyes were raspberry-colored in the light. Gold's eyes were bright and sharp like a big cat's. And Grey's eyes were, well, grey.

"May I have the key?" Gold asked, reaching out. She clearly expected me to hand it over. I think she was used to being in charge.

I reached into my pocket, ready to be helpful and give it to her, but Bird got to my palm just as my fingers touched the enamel of the key. He began pecking between my fingers. *Don't you give them that key.*

"Ow! No. I mean, well. No." Satisfied, Bird stopped pecking and fluttered back to my shoulder.

"No?" Gold tilted her head and looked more puzzled than put out.

"That's our key!" Grey howled in her gravelly voice.

Pink cried some more.

I thought about lying to the witches but had no idea what lie to tell. Or even what to lie about. So I went for the truth instead. "No, I can't give you the key. The bird on my shoulder told me not to. And until I know what kind of witches you are, I think I'll just play it safe." I thought some more about what I knew of witches. "Besides, I need some leverage in case you try to eat me."

Gold nodded, as if it all made perfect sense. "Fair enough. But would you be so kind as to open the door and let us in? And tell us, child, why are you here?"

I decided to keep going with the truth. "The Clackity sent me to find my aunt Desdemona in exchange for the ghost of John Jeffrey Pope."

Something in what I said got the trio's full attention. Pink even stopped crying.

"Well, then. You don't have much time. And we should get inside." Gold glanced around, jumpy now, even though I knew she couldn't see much or far. Her being worried made me worried too. Getting inside was sounding better and better.

Closer to the second house, I saw it wasn't shimmering as much as it was flickering. The old-fashioned candy covering the walls—gumdrops and lemon drops and root beer barrels and countless ropes of black and red licorice—came in and out of focus, solid one moment and nearly transparent the next. Behind the candy facade were rough, moldy-looking boards and sticks.

The sparkling cottage was an illusion, and I knew just who and what that illusion was for.

I didn't think the witches would eat me, but I needed insurance. I slowed down a little as I neared the house, and thought about Lily, and that made me think about her lessons, and that gave me an idea.

I took off my backpack, opened it, and dug through it until I found what I was looking for. The small plastic container was still there, the lid sealed tight. I popped it open and flashed the contents to the three witches. I was gambling on their eyesight being as bad as Lily's.

"Holly berries and mistletoe," I announced as I shoved

the gooseberries and currants into my mouth as quickly as possible. They were warm and sweating from a full day in my backpack, but still tasted okay. As I choked down as many as I could, I thought, *This had better work or I might be in trouble.*

"Girl, what are you doing?" Grey demanded.

"You'll be sick—die!" Gold was horrified.

"You'll taste terrible!" Pink lamented.

"*Aha!* I *knew* you were going to eat me! But now, if you do, you'll get sick. I'm . . . I'm immune to mistletoe and holly berries, but I bet you're not." I hoped I sounded more confident than I felt, which was not very confident at all. Plus, I felt a little queasy from the warm berries hitting my empty stomach all at once.

"Well played, girl." Grey was begrudgingly impressed. She stood a little too close to me on the front steps and I retreated a bit toward the door. With her thin smirk of a smile, Grey could have *been* Lily. I was suddenly home-sick to my bones. But if I didn't find Aunt Des and get her out of this place, there wouldn't be a home to go back to. I had to push away the thought because that tight little ball was back between my shoulders and now was definitely not the time to freak out.

At the door I pulled the key from my pocket. There was a lock the size of an apple hanging from a latch. It was decorated with the same candy-cane enamel as the key. The three witches huddled around me, watching. They made me nervous, standing close like that. And when I got nervous, I forgot how to do simple things. Like use keys.

"Please step back," I said as politely as I could. "I'm still not sure you don't want to eat me, and you're also making me very self-conscious."

The witches murmured and muttered and grumbled, but they took two steps back. Here's the thing: witches might eat you, but other than that, they generally respected your boundaries.

I slid the key into the lock and the mechanism turned with a satisfying clunk. Then I pushed the door wide to find that it opened into a narrow, and very long, hallway. It was far too long a hallway for the small cottage to contain, but as it wasn't even the sixth-strangest thing to happen that day, I didn't spend too much time thinking about it.

What interested me more than the hallway itself were the paintings hanging on the walls. Along each side of the hall was a perfect line of dozens and dozens of portraits. They were all of children, and they were terrible. Not terrible in a frightening way, although they were kind of scary, but terrible in a "whoever painted these is not exactly a naturally gifted or formally trained artist" sort of way.

Under each painting was a small, rectangular piece of paper. There were first names, which I assumed belonged to the children in the bad paintings. Under the names were what could only have been cooking instructions.

They looked something like this:

~Jimmy~
Rosemary, thyme, a pinch of sage

Lightly salted (no pepper)
Olive oil drizzle to finish

From behind me, Pink asked in an eager voice, "Do you like them? I painted them all myself. I have a bit of a gift, I must admit."

"They are . . . um . . . they're remarkable." It wasn't a lie.

Grey made a sound somewhere between disapproval and disgust.

I could almost hear Pink blush even pinker as she replied, "Thank you, dear. Not everyone appreciates my talent."

The witches had recipes—recipes for *kids*—hanging all over their walls. I seriously thought about turning around and making a run for the front door. But as I walked down the hallway and plotted my escape, the trio of witches close behind, I noticed something interesting. Mixed in with the portraits of the children, occasional paintings of animals began to take their place. Soon there were almost no children at all, and paintings of vegetables began to appear. By the time we reached the end of the hallway, nearly all the paintings were of gourds and zucchini and mushrooms. There were very few animals and not a single child.

I turned to face the witches. "Are you going *vegetarian*?"

"Yes," said Gold.

"Harrumph," harrumphed Grey.

"Mostly," said Pink.

"I know a vegetarian witch!"

"You do not," argued Grey. "There's only one vege-tarian witch we know of in the area, and she wouldn't cavort with the likes of you."

"Shush, sister," Gold told Grey. Then, still without her glasses, she leaned in close to better see me. "And how is it you know Lillian Littleknit?"

That was when I learned that the witches didn't trust me any more than I trusted them. Gold was testing me, even if she was smiling prettily while she was doing it.

"It's not *Lillian* Littleknit, it's Lilith. And she prefers to be called Lily. Anyone who knows her would know that."

Grey gave me an approving *harrumph*. Gold nodded. And Pink actually clapped. It appeared I'd passed the test. After that, something changed in the air between me and the trio. Maybe it was that by knowing Lily we all had something in common, or maybe we didn't see each other as threats anymore. And there was something kind of nice about somehow sharing a friend—it made home feel a little less far away. Either way, the hard little ball between my shoulders was gone. Even Bird was calm.

"Let's go to the kitchen and chat," suggested Gold.

Pink added, "And we probably weren't going to eat you anyway, but now that we know you're a friend of Lily's, you have our word we won't."

It was about the best I could hope for. I thought maybe these three would be able to tell me something useful before I left, and it seemed more likely they would help me if we were on good terms. "Thanks for not eating me. Oh, and by the way, I'm—"

"No names!" yelped Grey.

"Let's not exchange names, darling," said Gold. Her face was gentle, but her eyes were serious, and maybe a little scared.

Pink covered her ears and hummed loudly.

"Why not?" I asked the question as we sat down at a large wooden table in the center of the spacious kitchen. Herbs hung from hooks in the ceiling, plants grew on sunny windowsills, and I could smell bread baking in the old-fashioned iron stove. "And who's making bread?"

"I am," Pink said proudly. "It's been cooking since we locked ourselves out of the house. I'm sure it's ready now." She crossed the room, grabbed a thick towel, and pulled a golden-brown loaf of bread out of the oven.

I started to ask how it was possible the bread had been baking for a month. Then I remembered, *Witches*, and didn't bother.

Gold answered my first question. "Names are powerful things. With a name, you can enter into a contract, or acquire a debt. With a name you have power over a person."

"Not to mention," Grey added as she stepped out of the room, "if we don't know your name, we can't say for sure we've met you if someone were to come looking for you. Our eyes, you know, they aren't very good."

I thought about that. The Clackity seemed to be keeping tabs on me, so it wouldn't need to ask. There was no one else here to come looking for me. Except, maybe, John Jeffrey Pope. And something told me this trio of sisters would be more than a match for Pope.

Grey returned with a handful of eyeglasses, giving a pair each to Pink and Gold and keeping a pair for herself. In their glasses, their resemblance to Lily was undeniable.

Pink brought a platter with hot, crusty bread and little bowls of herbed butter to the table. I reached back and touched Bird lightly. He tapped back, *Eat. It's okay.*

"Do all witches look alike?" I asked around a mouthful of the best bread I'd ever eaten. It was so good I didn't worry much about what else had been cooked in that oven.

"That's a very rude question," Grey said between bites.

"Not at all," answered Gold, "but cousins often do."

"Lily is your cousin? Then why do you live here"—I gestured around the room—"and she lives out there?"

"It isn't a very exciting story," Gold began. "Our mothers had a spat, as sisters will."

"It was . . . political differences," Grey said.

"Our mother is wicked," Pink added. "A bad, wicked witch. She was banished—"

"It *isn't* a very exciting story," Gold repeated firmly, staring hard at Pink.

Pink stopped talking. Her cheeks grew even pinker, and her glasses fogged up as her eyes watered with hurt feelings or embarrassment. I couldn't tell which, but I felt sorry for her either way. I got the feeling she said the wrong thing, or made silly mistakes, a lot. And that made me want to protect her, or at least be extra nice to her.

The silence in the kitchen was uncomfortable, and we all filled it by eating more bread.

Grey was the first to speak. "So, girl, what is your aunt doing here on our side of the field? And why is it you've been sent for her?"

I explained again about meeting The Clackity and the deal it had made with me. "And I'm not sure why Aunt Des was in the abattoir, except it could have been for The Clackity. Or it could have been for Pope. She's an expert on the paranormal and otherworldly," I added in case it mattered.

Grey rolled her eyes. She wasn't impressed.

Gold shook her head. "I know that Clackity creature. It's old. It has outlived everything it's ever known, and the outliving has made it . . . unpredictable."

"That's not living," cut in Grey. "Girl, Clackity is a ghost as sure as Pope is, but it's spent too much time lingering between one side and the other. The lingering's made the creature completely mad. Pope is younger, and stronger. And a different kind of bad. They're both dangerous alone, but you don't want to bring them together."

My heart started to beat triple time. The whole reason I was here was to get Des and take Pope back to The Clackity, to keep up my end of our fair, good deal. If I couldn't do that, how was I supposed to make everything right? I rubbed my hands on my jeans. "But my aunt. This is how I get her back. I go through all seven houses and—"

"All seven houses?" The look on Gold's face frightened me.

"Yes. All seven. In order. No cheating. Clackity said

the houses wouldn't let me." My voice was shaking a little and I couldn't stop it.

"Oh, girl," said Pink sadly. "I liked you so much before I knew you were going to die."

Going to die. Pink's words made me very still and very quiet, like if I didn't move or breathe, they couldn't find me and come true.

"Hush, sister," said Grey. "Girl, it's time for you to go. I wish we could tell you what to expect. . . ."

"But the houses are different for everyone," said Gold.

"Except the last one," corrected Grey.

"And this one," added Pink.

"We can help a bit, I think." Grey stood up and pushed her heavy glasses up her nose.

Gold nodded. "A gift from each of us. How you use them is up to you." She reached into the deep pockets of her yellow dress and pulled out a single match. It was iridescent black, and as long as a chopstick. "Take this. You can use it only once, so use it well."

"Thank you." I took the match, not knowing what to do next.

Pink rummaged around in a drawer near the stove until, with an "Aha," she found what she was looking for. I heard what she held before I saw it. She smiled her sweet pink smile as she placed a tiny bell in my hand. It glowed rose gold and hung from a delicate matching chain. I thought I could feel it vibrating just the littlest bit, like it was excited to be used.

"This is magic," she said softly, like it was a secret between the two of us, and not something someone would expect of a gift given by a witch. "I enchanted it myself. Wear it when you want to be very quiet."

The bell jingled loudly, louder than such a tiny bell should. I thanked Pink and took the bell and held it in my hand next to the match.

Grey stared at me for a beat. I could see she was deciding something. Then she nodded curtly, having come to a decision only she knew about. She walked to the windowsill and plucked the single small flower from a white ceramic pot. Its petals were dove grey, its center rose pink, and its stem and leaves golden yellow. She dropped the flower into a small paper sack and handed it to me. Then she grasped my wrist and pulled me close, whispering so the others couldn't hear. "This is for Mother," she said in a low, low voice. "When you meet her, and I am afraid you will, you give this to her. Do you understand?"

Eyes wide, I nodded.

"Good." Grey squeezed my arm the very same way Lily would. The squeeze said, *Be brave, be smart, you can do this.*

As Grey released my arm, there was a knock at the front door. Three slow—almost lazy—raps. All three sisters spun to look down the long hall to the door at the end of it.

"That will be Pope," said Gold.

"Let's get ready, then," sighed Grey.

"I love this part," giggled Pink.

Each sister ran her hands over her hair and clothes and across her face. The transformation was subtle. All of them had been pretty before, but after a few waves and flicks, they were lovely. Beautiful, actually.

"We can't harm him any more than he can harm us," said Gold over her shoulder as she started up the hallway.

"But we can sure distract him." Pink was radiant.

Grey took me again by the arm to the back door. As we walked, I put the sisters' gifts into my backpack. Grey shoved a chunk of bread into my hand. "Eat while you walk. It's hungry work you'll be doing." She patted my shoulder. "And it is good fortune to have this little one with you."

Bird puffed up as big as he could under her compliment.

I did not want to leave the warm kitchen and the weird sisters. I didn't know what to say, and my throat was all tight and scratchy, so I threw my arms around Grey and held her tight.

Grey accepted the hug, even though she didn't hug me back. "Go now," she said. "Go and save your aunt. And please remember to give Mother my gift. And, child? Hurry. I don't know how long my sisters can distract the creature who's after you."

I nodded and wiped my eyes as Grey gently pressed me out the back door. I heard the lock clank behind me.

I was well on my way down the path, the licorice trees slowly losing ground to the mixed-up forest from before, when I remembered I still had the candy-cane key in my pocket along with the brass key from not-my-house. I almost turned back to return it to the sisters but thought of Pope behind me and Desdemona ahead of me and kept going.

12

The mixed-up forest was quiet, but not silent.
There were sounds, deep in the woods past where my
eyes could reach. Sounds that told me Bird and I weren't
alone. There was chirping and chittering of bats and
birds. And creeping noises of movement, leaves and
branches shifting and being pushed aside by bigger animals. At least, I hoped they were just animals.

Something edged close enough to the path for me to
see the texture of its grey pelt and the tips of its pert ears.
It was the little fawn, and he was still clear-eyed. Not a
trace of The Clackity to be found. The fawn would prance
ahead and then circle back behind us, never straying far.
I liked having him close.

As I walked, I chewed on the last of the good bread
from the witches' house. Even without the herbed butter
it was delicious and, somehow, still warm and steaming. I
felt better than I had since stepping into the abattoir. I had
freed the little fawn with the help of Bird. And I had two
houses behind me, and neither of them had been all *that*
bad. Not really, not when my imagination told me there
was so much more The Clackity could put in my way.

I thought about what Pink said, the thing about me dying. But she seemed to say a lot of things that weren't quite right. If Grey had said it, I'd be a little—a lot—more worried. At least, that was what I told myself. Sometimes we tell ourselves things that aren't entirely true until they start to feel like they really are. I guess I do, anyway.

Then I thought about what I had going for me. I had two keys and a bird on my shoulder, and sometimes I had a little grey fawn. I had friends in a candy house. I didn't have the prickly-neck feeling that came from Pope watching me, and Bird was so calm he might have even been asleep. The whole quest began to feel . . . possible.

As I thought and ate and walked, I felt a shift in the air around me. Something was different, but I couldn't say just what it was. At first it seemed the sky was lightening, but upon closer inspection it was exactly the same infected shade it had been all day. No, the sky was the same, but the forest was changing again. It was thinning out, allowing more of the unlikely black sunlight to filter through. It was no longer endless woods to my right and to my left. The trees were shallower now and seemed almost planned in the way they lined the path.

The path was changing too. Through the forest, it had been mostly dirt with the occasional rock and tree root, uneven enough that I could never entirely stop paying attention to what might be coming next. At some point in the last stretch, the path had become pebbled with round gravel, and even as I realized that, the texture changed again. It had become a proper cobblestone walkway, four feet across. As I watched and walked, the cobblestones began to give way to familiar pavement. Soon, almost like it had never been an uneven dirt path, the route before me was paved, black and smooth.

I was trying to decide whether all this changing was a good or a bad thing when, from behind me, came the clattering of small hooves. It made me jump a little—I guess I was more nervous than I'd thought—and I turned to see the grey fawn on the path. He'd stopped and was prancing in place just short of where the pavement began. He stretched a hesitant hoof out over the pavement but jerked it back before it made contact. He was coming no farther. The fawn belonged in the woods, or *to* them, not to whatever this next place would be. He made a mewling noise I didn't know fawns could make. I wasn't sure whether he was telling me to come back or saying goodbye.

I jogged the few paces back to him and rested my palm, and Bird, between his ears. "I hope I get to see you again." And I meant it. I scratched between his ears as I whispered. I didn't like leaving him behind but felt sure he didn't belong where I was going. With one final pat on the head, I left the fawn and turned back toward the paved path. After only a few steps I could hear him dancing away, and then a rustling as he left the path and returned to the woods.

I didn't look back.

Bird and I pressed on.

Before long, the light around me really did change, and it had nothing to do with the black sun and purple sky. Off either side of the path, streetlights emerged from behind the trees. They flickered a pale yellow, breaking up the solid skyline, but not doing much to brighten it. The light from the lamps was swallowed by the sky before it could even reach the ground.

The streetlights were set evenly in well-kept green-black grass, like they would be in any neighborhood. And as in any neighborhood, there were the silhouettes of houses set deep in lawns behind them.

You'd think it would be nice, being back in a regular-looking neighborhood. But it wasn't. Not at all. My heart pounded and panic fingers crawled up my neck and reached around my throat. My breathing got fast and shallow. This wasn't right. There was supposed to be a third house after the second, not a street lined with a dozen or more.

I stopped.

It was The Clackity.

It had changed the rules, and there would be more than the seven houses it had promised back in the abattoir.

I was beginning to hyperventilate and knew if I didn't move soon, I would freeze up, so I shook myself. I jogged across the first lawn toward the silhouette house. As I drew closer, the house stayed out of focus. It remained a two-story silhouette.

I slowed down and approached it with more caution.

Nearly at the front door, or where the front door should have been, I could see it wasn't a house at all. It was the right shape, but nothing else about it resembled a house. As flat and shallow as a sheet of paper, it had been cut from the strange sky like a home for a life-sized paper doll family.

With the purple sky sheared away to reveal what was behind it, I was faced with the deepest, thickest black I had ever seen. I stepped to the edge where the lawn was cut away and met the black. The very tips of my toes hung over the precipice as I looked out and down. Beyond and below was only black. There was no stars and no moon in that strange nothing night, but there was movement. The black shifted and churned like the shadows in the abattoir. I knew if I were to step over the edge I would fall straight down and never stop falling.

It was the most overwhelming, amazing, frightening thing I had ever seen. I was too awed to be scared. The black nothing was all I could think about. It was bigger than anything I could imagine, bigger than that day and bigger than my quest and bigger than my panic. And then I was thinking about how it was kind of beautiful, too.

I sat down then, on the edge of the lawn, and dangled my feet into the nothing. There, half in the black, it didn't feel cold or warm, damp or dry. It didn't feel like anything at all.

But it felt familiar, too, like it was a part of me.

I leaned forward, farther than I should have been able to without tipping over headfirst into the nothing. I bent almost in half to look under the edge of the earth and see what was there. It was nothing. Just more nothing-at-all.

There was a part of me—the part that wasn't hypnotized by the black nothing—that screamed to scoot back and away from the hole in space. But there was another part of me, a bigger part that was growing by the second, that was curious to know what all that falling would feel like.

I guess what scares me most about the whole thing is that I'm still not sure what choice I would have made if Bird hadn't been there. Would I have moved to safety, or would I have taken the leap? I don't like to think about it.

I wasn't sure how long he pecked at my neck and ears, but it was the pain of Bird's little beak that brought me back. I sat up and wiped my hand across the side of my neck to find it was sticky with drops of my own blood.

I did move then, and fast, because all of a sudden, my fuzzy brain cleared, and I was very afraid. My heart pounded so hard I could feel it in my eyeballs, and I thought I'd have to change my socks, my feet were so sweaty. If there was one thing I didn't like, it was heights. And I'd just been on the edge of the highest height I could imagine. I scooted back until I was ten feet away from the hole in the sky. I held my breath the whole time, until I was sure I was far enough away that I couldn't accidentally tumble forward and down when I finally managed to stand up.

I reached back with a trembling hand and stroked Bird, who had returned to his perch on my shoulder. I couldn't get any words out, but I knew he understood what I meant. *Thanks, buddy. That was close.*

I sat for a few minutes, slowly unwrapping the fingers of a panic attack from around my brain and lungs, recovering from whatever had happened to me at the edge of the sky. When I got up, my legs felt a little stiff and sore. I had no idea what time it was. Time, like everything else, didn't seem to follow the usual rules on this side of the green-black field. I just knew it had already been a very long day, and I still had a long way to go.

I returned to the paved walkway and continued down it, no longer tempted to inspect the house-shaped holes that sat back on the deep lawns. I'd been offered a choice, and with Bird's help, I'd made the right one. No way was I going to be tempted again.

Far up ahead there was something in the middle of the path. As I got closer, I saw it was the third house—a beige little square of a structure, squat and low to the ground. This was the least interesting house I could ever remember seeing. It had a tiny front porch with potted plants on either side of the front door. The yellow flowers looked tired from too many days under the black sun, but they also looked like flowers you could find on any front porch anywhere. As boring as the house was, it was good to be there despite all of The Clackity's tricks.

I walked up the three steps to the front door and almost grabbed the handle before I remembered I didn't have the key. I wasn't worried . . . not *too* worried, anyway. This was such a simple house, I just knew the key would be simple to find.

And I was right.

It was beneath the second potted plant I looked under. The key was small and steel, as nondescript as the house.

I sighed, thinking this one might not be too bad. I mean, how could it be, after I'd already survived an invisible fire and a trio of witches and almost jumping into a bottomless void? I slipped the key into the lock, turned the handle, and opened the door.

13

The white door opened without a sound, not even the slightest squeak of hinges. I stood on the threshold looking in as I added the silvery key to the collection in my pocket. Behind the front door was exactly one room: a smallish room as square and as beige as the third house itself. In the room there were no rugs, no art, no furniture.

No anything.

There were two more white doors, spaced evenly across the back wall. I stepped into the room and let go of the front door. Fast, like it had been pulled, but without a sound, the front door shut behind me.

And then it was gone.

Where the front door had been moments ago was now more beige wall. My heart hammered in protest and I balled my hands into tight fists. I did not like being trapped anywhere.

But you're not trapped, I told myself with a deep breath. *You have two doors. Pick one.*

So I did. I rubbed my hands on my jeans, shook out my cramped fingers, and picked the door on the right. I didn't have any good reason for choosing it—maybe it was just because I was right-handed.

I stepped into another square beige room with two doors on the back wall. The right door, the one I had come through, was now in the center of the wall, because it had become the only door. I peeked back out to see that the left door was still there, in the other room, where it was supposed to be. Where it led, I had no idea, but it was a different room than the right door was taking me to. The effect of being between the two rooms was disorienting, and my head swam a little as I tried to make it make sense. It was like looking at an M. C. Escher picture for too long—eventually, your brain hurts from trying to work it out.

I stepped through the right door, and it closed behind me and disappeared. With two new doors to choose from, again I picked the door on the right. This door had the tiniest imperfection near its handle, a chip in the paint that exposed the wood beneath.

I stepped through the door into another square room, another set of doors to choose from. I kept choosing the doors on the right. I was making progress, but toward what, I wasn't sure. I couldn't shake that boxed-in feeling, but as long as I kept moving, I was going to be okay.

I must have opened and closed ten doors. When I reached for the next handle of the next right door, something stopped me cold. My stomach dropped and felt like it was full of icy marbles and my heart started climbing back to its favorite place in my throat.

There was a chip in the paint near the handle that exposed the wood beneath.

"It can't be." But it was. In my heart, I knew it was. I traced my finger along the imperfection. Somehow, I was back in the room with the chipped door.

I sat down on the hardwood floor, my back against the wall between the doors. I needed to stay calm if I was going to figure this out. If I panicked and froze, I'd be stuck here forever, and Pope was somewhere behind me and Aunt Desdemona would be trapped in the bone house and no one would ever know what happened to us and . . .

Breathe. Focus. Breathe. Focus, focus, focus.

I took a deep, slow, shaking breath. I needed to look at something other than beige walls and white doors. I needed to *do* something. So I opened my backpack to inventory what I had in there.

I had:

a black hoodie
two bottles of water
a granola bar
the black eyeliner from Aunt Des (the kind in a
    plastic tube, not the pencil kind that needed
    a sharpener)
my aunt's black purse
a long black match (from Gold)
a tiny rose-gold bell on a chain (from Pink)
a paper bag with a still-fresh pink, gold, and grey
    flower inside (from Grey)

Inside my aunt's purse, there was:

a vial of white salt
a vial with something thicker than water—
    maybe oil—and a dropper in the lid
a tiny New Testament Bible
a pair of giant cat-eye sunglasses
Aunt Desdemona's favorite red lipstick
a spare house key
a sleek black mirrored compact

That was it.

I sat and stared at the odd little collection for a while, hoping for inspiration. There had to be something here that could help me navigate through this trap of a house. As far as I could tell, it was all just a useless pile of junk.

I got up and started pacing.

From the middle of the room, I stared at the doors in front of me. There was nothing about either of them to tell me what might be behind them. I would have to just try doors, one after the other, until I figured out the right combination. What I couldn't figure out was how to keep track. I knew I'd be confused in no time.

Bird tapped me gently on my shoulder. *Time to move.*

"I know, buddy." I reached back and patted the little tattoo creature. I wondered absently if he would stay with me. For better or worse, this day would eventually be over. I wondered if I would be marked forever.

Marked.

Duh.

I needed to mark the doors as I went through them.

I repacked my bag with everything but the eyeliner and slung the backpack over my shoulders.

I'd picked the door on the right last time, so now I chose the left. I marked it with a small black *X* in the center of the door and went through. In the next room I chose the right door and marked it with an *X*. In the next room I chose the right door, marked it, and was returned to the room with the chip on the right door and the black *X* on the left.

Under the *X*, I wrote *yes* and walked through. In the next room, I did the same, writing *yes* under the *X* on the right door. In the third room, the one that sent me back to the beginning, I wrote *no* under the *X* and *yes* on the left door.

This was going to work.

More than once, I got bounced back to the room with the chipped paint and the first black *X*. But now it wasn't scary when it happened. My plan was working just like it was supposed to. I just needed to be patient, keep my head clear, and get through the house. My heart was racing in my ears, but that was from the excitement of solving the puzzle. I was honestly feeling pretty proud of myself.

In the twelfth room, I marked the right door and paused before opening it. For just a moment, I thought I'd heard something behind the door. It was a shuffling sort of movement, like feet sliding on a hardwood floor.

I got very still and pressed my ear against the door. It was quiet on the other side, but it was a full sort of quiet.

Like someone was in there, holding their breath, pressing their ear against the door just an inch away from mine.

I had exactly two choices: freeze or make progress. I couldn't wait any longer.

I dug down as deep as I could and threw open the door and stepped through.

It didn't return me to the chipped-paint room. I'd made it into the next room.

Only this one wasn't empty.

As the door swung open into the thirteenth room, I was hit hard with the cave—*grave*—smell I'd noticed way back when I'd first stepped into the green-black field. The room was exactly like the twelve before it.

Except, of course, for the woman standing stone-still, facing the corner.

Her clothes were old-fashioned but didn't look old. The woman's ash-blond hair was cut in a short bob, and her peach-colored dress floated at her knees. Even from the back she looked glamorous in a black-and-white-photo sort of way. I immediately thought *flapper*, although I wasn't sure that was quite right.

Like the two of us were linked, as I stepped into the room, the woman turned around to face me. For a long moment I didn't understand what I was seeing—there was something wrong with her otherwise pretty face.

After a beat, I realized she had coins over her eyes. Copper coins small enough that I could still see some of the fringe of the long lashes that framed her eyes. Eyes that were hidden under the coins. Under the pennies.

The Clackity's words rolled over me like a wave.

Pretty Penny.

Lucky Penny.

Penny Dreadful.

I had the crazy thought the woman could see me, even with her eyes covered, because of those pennies. And because you only put pennies on dead people's eyes, chances were the lady standing in front of me *was* dead.

A ghost.

Living in Blight Harbor had taught me all sorts of things about death. A long time ago, people believed the coins would pay their loved one's way to the other side after they passed. Not so long ago, people used coins to keep the eyes of the dead from popping open at unexpected times. And who could blame them? It would be super creepy to suddenly have Uncle Frank staring at you after he'd died a day or two ago. In Blight Harbor, it was still a pretty common practice. And people did it for both reasons, depending on who you asked.

The penny-eyed ghost woman turned back around and walked to the door on the right. Her steps were clipped and uneven, like her shiny white shoes didn't fit properly. At the door, she held up a gloved hand and knocked three times. The raps were soft, but they echoed like she was in a huge, open cathedral instead of a small, square room.

The woman cocked her head and waited. When enough time had passed, she hobbled over to the door on the left. Watching her walk made me sad for her. She should have been graceful and light in her party clothes instead of limping and dragging her feet across the floor.

At the door on the left, she knocked again. Three times. And waited. This time, she didn't have to wait long. From the other side of the door came three slow knocks, like an answer to her question.

The woman turned to face me and beckoned me with a gloved hand. *Follow me.*

I reached over my shoulder and tapped Bird. I whispered, "What do you think, buddy?"

Bird beat his wings slow and steady, but he didn't move from his perch. *I don't know. You must decide.*

As I thought it over, the woman tensed and turned her coin-covered gaze over my shoulder. She was like an animal that hears something it doesn't trust and freezes just before it runs. She beckoned me again, more urgently this time. She was scared.

I noticed then that her gloves, like her shoes, didn't fit properly. They were filled by her thumb, pointer, and middle fingers. But her ring fingers and pinkies seemed to be missing, the gloves empty and hanging where the fingers should have been.

She had lost some of her fingers. Or someone had taken them from her.

I would have bet everything she was missing toes as well.

I knew then that I was not afraid of this poor, dead woman. But I *was* afraid of whatever it was that was scaring her. So I made a decision.

She held the door open for me, and I went through. As I passed her, I got a good look at the pennies on her eyes. They were shiny and new-looking, but on the left one, under the head of Abraham Lincoln, I could see the date: 1921. That was all the confirmation I needed.

In the doorway, between the two rooms, I stopped and took her hand in mine. Through her gloves, I could feel where her fingers were missing. The part of her hand she still had was cold as granite in the winter. I could see tears seeping out of her covered eyes, falling slowly from below the pennies.

I wanted to tell her I was sorry, that I was going to try to make it better. That I would keep John Jeffrey Pope from hurting anyone else, keep him from hurting Aunt Des. But I didn't know whether it was true, whether I really could. And I didn't want to lie to her. So I didn't say anything at all.

Somewhere, behind us, a door slammed shut.

Someone had joined us in the little beige house.

The prickly-neck feeling was back.

Pope.

Moving quickly now, the woman pulled me by the

hand into the next room. There was a dark-haired man there, standing in the corner. His clothes, like my guide's, were old-fashioned, but not old. And when he turned to face us, he had pennies over his eyes. He was missing fingers under his gloves too.

He limped to the door on the right and knocked three times. This time it was the correct door, and there were three knocks in return. The man opened the door for us, and the woman led me to the next room.

As we passed through, the man nodded. *You're welcome. Keep moving. Be brave.*

The man didn't follow us. He stayed in his room. As the door closed on its own behind me, I saw him return to his corner.

Behind us, another door slammed.

Pope was coming.

But how was he working it out so quickly?

How did he know which doors to use?

Because, I realized in horror.

Because I'd done the work for him.

I'd marked the doors, so carefully and so clearly. In my effort not to get lost, I'd left him a trail better than any fairy-tale bread crumbs.

My stomach sank as low as it ever had and my shoulders tightened up so much I thought they might touch. I wanted to bury my face in my hands so no one could see the red I knew was burning in my cheeks. But we didn't have time for me to feel sorry for myself, to feel stupid, to panic. We had to move.

The woman and I worked our way through eight more

rooms. Men and women in corners, pennies over their eyes, fingers missing from their gloves. Each knocked a question, and an answer was knocked in return. Each then held the proper door for us, and each nodded as we passed.

Every time we passed through a door, another one slammed somewhere behind us. Each time, the sound was a little closer than the one before. Pope was gaining on us. I knew what The Clackity had promised, *safe in houses*. But I wasn't sure why I should believe the creature from the abattoir. Clackity had already spied on me through the dolls in not-my-house. It had tried to scare me by using the poor fawn and had tried to trick me with the silhouette houses and the black void. Any trust I had in The Clackity had slipped away.

A petite woman with an oversized hat held the door for us, and my guide and I entered a room that was larger than the rest. The small woman slipped back into the other room, and without thinking, I pulled the door shut behind me. The room had windows on the far wall that looked out at the black sun and purple sky, and a single door stood between them. In the center of the room was a long wooden table. It had space and chairs enough to seat a dozen people.

Maybe, I thought, *this is where the penny-eyed ghosts have dinner every night and talk about their day.* I knew the idea was silly. It was just my rational brain and my panic fighting one another for space in my head. I pushed the thought away and focused on the man standing in the corner.

He was very tall, nearly too tall for the room, and very thin. He was dressed all in black, and the top of his black hat almost met the ceiling. He did not turn around.

My guide went to a chair on the side of the table near one end, the end farthest from the man, and sat down. She gestured for me, but I didn't want to sit. I wanted to get out the back door and go to the next house.

Mostly, I just wanted out of *this* house.

Bird began to get anxious, his wings flicking rhythmically on my back like tapping fingers.

"I know, buddy. We're going to go soon."

I was working up the nerve to move around the table and out the door, staying as far away from the tall man as possible, when he turned around.

He turned quickly, but his clothes lagged just a half second behind him. Like they weren't really clothes at all, but something loose and alive. He had a pale, pale face, and only one eye was covered by a penny. The other eye was sewn shut with black thread and rough stitches.

The man grinned at me with a mouth full of sharp and broken teeth. I was so tired of that grin.

I started making a plan, then decided not to think about it so I wouldn't chicken out.

I charged the Clackity man with my hand out.

Bird knew what to do.

He flew into my palm as I moved across the room. I was going to send Clackity away and out of this man. The same way I had with the fawn.

But he was fast. And maybe he expected it this time, because before I was halfway across the room, the man was in the opposite corner. I couldn't tell how he'd moved so quickly, but those weird clothes trailed just behind him. Almost like a shadow.

The man's grin spread just a little wider. "Girl child," he croaked. "Pretty Penny. Let's have a sit and talk. We will sit here, by this charming lady, and the girl child can sit all the way over there. That will make her feel safer. And The Clackity, too."

The Clackity meant for us to sit at opposite sides of the table from one another, each at a far end. I didn't like the idea of him sitting so close to my guide, but I didn't want him any closer to me. I was trying to sort out what to do, how to protect us both, when there was a slamming of a door in the room behind us.

There was a sure stomping of heavy shoes in the other room, so different from the sliding and shuffling of the broken-footed ghosts. I wasn't sure why he didn't charge through the door then and there, and I thought, *Maybe he doesn't want to be close to Clackity any more than I do?* Not that I wanted Pope in the room with me, but I also didn't want him in there with his former victims. It was my worrying about the ghosts, about what Pope had done to them—what he might do to them now—that convinced me to talk to Clackity.

"Did he hurt them? The penny ghosts?"

The Clackity man sat at his end of the table and I sat at mine. He stretched out his long, gloved hands in a *What can you do?* sort of gesture. "Of course he hurt them. She's such a smart penny, we thought she'd sorted that out—"

"No," I snapped, cutting him off. "I don't mean a long time ago. I know Pope hurt those people a long time ago. I mean *now*. I mean is he hurting them again?"

The Clackity man shook his head. He made a face that was supposed to look solemn, but I could see its terrible smile just underneath. I didn't know if The Clackity was evil, or just broken, but it was enjoying this. And that made me even angrier. I used the anger because it turned into adrenaline and didn't leave any room for panic.

"Tell the truth. Is he hurting them?"

"No, Pretty Penny. The Cow and Piggy Man is done with those ghosties. He doesn't care for them. He doesn't like the coins on their eyes. The coins make it so he can't see them anymore. He's curious about Pretty Penny, though, and her auntie. But remember, the little girl child is safe in houses. Safe until the field."

"Why should I believe you? You're a liar, and you cheat. You said the houses wouldn't let me cheat, but *you* get to."

The Clackity man furrowed his brows in what looked like real confusion. "The Clackity doesn't cheat, and The Clackity does *not* lie. Sometimes there are truths The Clackity doesn't tell, but we never lied to our lucky penny."

It was then that I realized the room behind us had grown silent. Pope was being still. Was he thinking? Or listening? Either way, I was ready to get out of there.

I stood up and began to make my way closer to the Clackity man. I lowered my voice to a whisper as I moved, just in case Pope was listening, "Why don't you take him now? Just grab Pope and be done with it? Then

I can get my aunt, and we'll both have what we want." I remembered what Grey had said, that the two of them were more dangerous together, but I needed to distract Clackity.

I was close then, close enough to touch the poor ghost man with Clackity inside him.

Clackity tilted his head in a way that made him look almost like an earnest dog. "Penny, The Clackity isn't really here. Clackity is back in the sad and shadowy place. We're just visiting. That is why you must bring us the Cow and Piggy Man."

The knob on the door to the room behind us rattled softly.

I froze. I stopped breathing and thinking. I'm not even sure my heart was beating.

Pope was testing it, the only door left between me and him.

The knob twisted back and forth. Then it rattled as he tried harder, but the door didn't open. The same thing had happened in not-my-house, when he couldn't open the door there, either. It seemed maybe Pope couldn't open doors if I had closed them. The houses wouldn't let me cheat, but maybe they weren't against me either. If that was right, it was important to know.

The Clackity man was still gibbering. I was tired of hearing its riddles, and I still didn't trust it. I needed to get to the fourth house. So, before Clackity could begin to wonder why I might be so close, Bird and I reached out and grabbed his bare wrist just above his black gloves.

The Clackity man hissed like an animal and tried to

pull away, but only for a second. That was how long it took for Clackity to leave the man and go back to wherever the rest of it lived.

I made a half-gasp, half-scream noise as the man's head dropped like a rock, almost slamming into the table. It floated there, just above the surface, for three, four, five seconds. When the man raised his head again, one eye was still covered with a penny. The other eye was open. It was grey and cloudy, but the way it locked on my own eyes told me he could see through it.

He nodded once, and tipped his hat. *Thank you for getting rid of that thing. Thank you for getting it out of me.*

"You're welcome," I told him. I watched as my pretty guide placed one of her ruined gloved hands over one of his. She rested her head on his shoulder. They belonged together, and it made me happy and sad at the same time.

My guide squeezed the man's hand, then stood up. She beckoned me to follow her to the back door.

So I did.

I wanted to hug her, thought it might be weird, then did it anyway. She stood very still at first, but then she wrapped her cold, thin arms around me and hugged back. It was something, being hugged by a ghost. She wasn't solid, but she was *there*. Almost like wind trapped in a human-shaped balloon.

When I pulled away from her, I could see she was crying again. But this time, a little smile tugged at one corner of her mouth.

She took a step back and held out both hands, arms straight and fists clenched. *Pick one.*

I tapped her right hand.

She flipped it over and opened it, palm up. Resting on her glove was an impossible key. It was made from blue sea glass, twice the size of a regular key, and had swirls and ridges that looked like they'd been formed by centuries in gently moving water.

I gingerly took the key from her hand. It was stronger and more solid than it looked. It felt like a promise in my hand—a promise that I would make it to the next house. "Thank you."

My guide still held her left hand out, waiting for me to pick it, too.

I tapped her hand and she flipped it over and opened it. On her palm were two shiny wheat pennies. Something about them made my skin crawl, but I knew I needed to take them. I was in no position to turn down a gift.

Besides, Bird was pecking the back of my neck gently. *Take the coins.*

I put the key in my key pocket, and the pennies in my other pocket.

My guide took my face in both her hands and lowered her face to kiss my forehead with her cold, soft lips. Then she went back to the man at the table and stood behind him. They each lifted a hand. *Goodbye.*

Bird pecked lightly at my shoulder.

It was time for me to go.

15

I walked out the back door of the little beige house onto a white step, gritty with sand.

Ahead of me was a desert. Gold sand sparkled in the black sun. It reminded me, with a sharp stab to my chest, of something I'd forgotten all about. The memory flooded through every part of me, washing away all the adrenaline and replacing it with the heavy, heavy feeling of remembering my parents. Sometimes, if I wasn't careful, I almost drowned in those memories.

The gold sand under the black sun reminded me of the pyrite crystal my dad kept on his desk before our house burned.

Before everything changed.

Pyrite was pretty, and it looked enough like gold that its nickname was "fool's gold." It wasn't technically very valuable, but Dad always said it wasn't worthless. It was protective, was supposed to ward off negative energy. The crystal on his desk came from Desdemona, and even though Dad laughed a little when it showed up in the mail, he never got rid of it.

For all the good it did him.

Had Des known something was going to happen? Was that why she'd sent it the summer before the fire? Or was it just a very Desdemona gift? Had Des known something was going to happen to *her*? Except, this time, I was going to find her, make it right. Because no way was I going to lose Des, too.

I stared off a little longer, lost in the twists of memory that were all mixed up with this place. Little bits and pieces skittered through my mind. Here, the smell of my dad's famous pancakes, there the glint of the sun on my mom's beautiful hair, and woven throughout was the sound of the laughter that had filled our home most days.

When Bird nudged me with his wings, the flood of memories receded, and I surfaced. I took a deep breath and returned to my current predicament.

I walked down the three steps leading off from the back door into the sand. When I looked behind me, the little beige house was gone. All I could see was fool's gold sand in every direction.

I jangled the keys and coins in my pockets with damp hands, trying to decide what to do next. I thought heading straight forward was the best choice, but without the beige house as a landmark, I was already disoriented. Being lost wasn't at the very top of my list of fears, but it was up there. The glare coming off the sand made it hard to see, and my head was beginning to hurt.

I remembered Aunt D's giant black sunglasses and pulled them out of her purse. I grabbed a bottle of water while I was at it and downed most of it.

Maybe I should have felt ridiculous in those oversized glasses, but I didn't. Looking through them, it was like seeing what *she* saw. Seeing the world the way she did. It made me feel like she wasn't very far away. Everything was just a little clearer, a little more focused. *I* was more focused. And it was then that I saw something other than sand off in the distance.

Far ahead of me, a shape rose from the floor of the desert into the air, shining bright blue in all the black and gold. I remembered the fourth house—blue and covered in glass—and I knew where to go next.

I don't know how long it took me to get to the fourth house. Not as long as it should have, but it still took a while. Bird and I didn't have much to say to each other as we traveled, and my mind went back to wandering, remembering. I thought about a story my mom made up for me when I was too small to read my own bedtime stories—she'd even turned it into a homemade book, complete with drawings (my mom wasn't an artist, but she was pretty creative). It was about a little girl who wanted to find the loneliest place on earth, and one of the places she tried was the desert. I told myself that story as I walked. I knew every word, even though the book had been lost in the fire like everything else. I tried not to think about that part.

With my mom's story in my head, and my feet on sand like my dad's pyrite, my parents were kind of with me. But also, they had never been farther away. My heart was so big and full and broken I thought it might suffocate me.

I didn't feel like crying. Or screaming. So I talked to them, to my parents.

"I miss you guys. All the time. Some days, it isn't so bad. Other days . . . well, they're worse. If I get home—*when* I get home—I'm going to look for you. Because I don't think you're dead. I think you're . . . somewhere. But not dead. I promise I'm going to look for you. But first I have to find D. And when I get her, and we get home, we're going to look for you together."

The only answer I got was a comforting nuzzle from Bird.

The sun was getting hotter, and sweat ran down my face and under my sunglasses. I pushed them up and wiped at my eyes, telling myself it was just sweat that was burning them.

"I think she's been looking for you. Des, I mean. She doesn't talk about it much, but I know she doesn't think you're dead either. One time she said something to Lily I wasn't supposed to hear. She said we could find you if we knew how to look. Not *where*, but *how*. So she thinks you're somewhere, and so do I. We're going to find you, and when we do, I'll tell you all about this crazy day. I'll tell you all about Blight Harbor, too. And I'll tell you how good Des has been to me, how much she loves me and how much I love her. And I do. I love her a lot. She's not you guys, but she's wonderful. She saved me when you guys . . . when you left. She saved me from being alone, and she saves me from myself sometimes too. So now I have to save her. It's my turn.

"I miss you, you know? A lot. And love you. A lot."

Pretty soon I ran out of things to say, but my heart was back to its usual size and it didn't hurt so much anymore. It felt a little like praying, talking to Mom and Dad like that. And, kind of like praying, I was sure someone heard my words as I spoke them out loud.

The fourth house was taller than I remembered. Or maybe it was just perspective, now that it was all by itself in a flat landscape. The house was mostly windows of frosted blue glass. It looked like a people aquarium. Everything about it was straight and square, and it belonged somewhere warm where the air smelled like salt. Somewhere under a blue sky and yellow sun and close to a great, wide ocean.

There were no steps, just a white stone porch that rose an inch or two above the sand.

The front door was the same blue glass as the windows. There was no keyhole anywhere to be found, which was weird since I had a key that matched.

I tried the handle. When I turned it, there was a sound like pebbles made from glass tumbling around. I pushed open the door and it felt like it pushed back. At first I thought it was heavy, until I saw that something was stopping it from swinging open. There was no floor to the house, only more sand.

There were no rooms or walls or ceilings in the fourth house.

Only a beach.

I'd managed to open the door enough to squeeze through. Once inside—or outside?—I took a deep breath.

On one side of the door, in the desert, the air didn't move. Here, "inside" the fourth house, there was a breeze coming off the calm, shining water. It mostly smelled like every beach trip I'd ever taken, like sand and water and the plants growing just beneath the surface, the ones that wash up on shore and rot. But here, the rotten smell was strong. Like maybe some animals were rotting along with the plants. And the smell made me wonder what kind of creatures might be living in all that water. I was willing to bet most of them wouldn't be very friendly.

There was so much water it might have been an enormous lake, or a small sea, but it was dark under the black sun. Out in that obsidian water was a small island, and I knew that was where I had to go.

I remembered the door then, and how Pope couldn't seem to open what I closed. So I turned to shut it behind me. But when I reached out and touched the handle, the door collapsed in a gush of clear water. One second it was there; the next, it was a puddle being sucked up by the greedy sand.

My head spun. I was inside a house that wasn't a house, and I couldn't get out because the door was gone. It was like a riddle where the words kept changing, and I couldn't keep up.

Looking past where the door had been, out toward the desert, I could make out a figure through the shimmering heat waves. It was too small and far away for me to see clearly, but I didn't need to.

It was Pope. Which meant it was time for me to go.

I didn't know what he could see. Was the blue house

still there for him, or could he see me standing there looking back at him? He was always behind me, but just out of reach. I didn't know if The Clackity was keeping him away or if he was making a game out of my not very fun-filled day.

I wasn't going to wait around to find out. I needed to get to that island, put some distance and some water between us.

Down at the edge of the beach, I saw a few interesting things. There was a huge piece of driftwood, but where it could have come from, I had no idea. There wasn't a tree, or any other growing thing, in sight. There was also a small rowboat. It was shiny with black paint and was pulled half into the sand, where it rocked gently in the water lapping the shore. If I was going to get to the island, it seemed I had three options:

(a) I could swim.

Not a chance.

(b) I could use the driftwood to float.

Nope.

Or

(c) I could take the rowboat.

Yup.

I didn't exactly know how to row a boat, but the idea of getting into that dark water was out of the question. So the rowboat it was.

"Let Pope swim," I said. "Maybe he'll drown."

Bird ruffled his feathers in agreement.

I didn't know whether ghosts *could* drown, had no idea what the rules were about that kind of thing.

Desdemona would know. I'd have to remember to ask her. My list of questions for D was growing.

Stepping into the rowboat was easy; pushing it off the soggy shore was not. I freed an oar and tried to shove off, but the sand pulled back, like it didn't want to let the boat go. I climbed out, back onto the beach, and tried to push the boat into the water, thinking that maybe without my weight it would move. It still bobbed a little with the tide, but it didn't budge.

I was sweating and saying words I knew Des wouldn't approve of, so I got back into the boat and started hacking at the ground with the oar. Sand flew all around. It speckled my sunglasses and got in my mouth. It was salty. And greasy. And gross. I spit out as much as I could, but I could still taste it.

Attempting to beat the beach to death with an oar accomplished exactly nothing.

I couldn't move the boat.

That hard ball was back between my shoulders, and I was having trouble breathing despite the wide-open space and the breeze. My lungs were as deflated as old birthday party balloons.

I sat heavily on the bench in the rowboat and put my head in my hands. Frustration piled up on me, and even Bird was silent. We were both out of ideas. It was such a bizarre problem, but it was still a problem.

"At this rate, I should just go back out to the desert and meet Pope halfway."

Bird pecked my collarbone. Hard. He didn't think I was funny.

Focus.

I took a deep breath and lifted my head.

I looked at the boat, really *looked* at it, for the first time. It was like I imagined any rowboat would be, except I didn't think they were usually painted lacquer black. It was small, but big enough for me and my back-pack and one other person on the second bench. There was nothing else in it, except the sand I'd dragged in on my shoes.

I ran my hands over the edges of the boat, and when I got to the front—the bow, right?—I saw something I had missed before. There was a small plaque embedded in the wood at the very tip of the boat. It was painted the same black as everything else, which was why I had missed it in the first place. On the plaque, stamped into the metal, was just one word.

HURRY.

And under that word was what looked suspiciously like a keyhole.

I fished the sea-glass key out of my pocket and held my breath as I tried it.

It fit and turned.

The key had never been for the house at all—it was for the boat.

No engine roared to life, which was disappointing. Instead the plaque popped up like the lid to a jewelry box, which was *not* disappointing. Inside was a compartment with another key. This one was made of twigs, with tiny green-black leaves still attached.

It looked like this:

I reached in and gently pulled the key free. It looked so delicate, like it would crumble in my hand. When I did, the boat moved. Except that wasn't right. It didn't just move. It was *pulled*, like strong hands were yanking it from the shore and into the water. I almost lost my balance, and the wooden key, but managed to keep them both and sat back down on the nearest of the two benches. I put both keys—the sea glass and the twigs—in my pocket with the others.

The boat pulled away from the shore and out into the dark water. It wasn't fast, but it was steady, and I was moving toward the island. The oars dragged through the water, motionless. They left a narrow wake behind them.

It was the first time that day I didn't feel much of anything, no panic or fear or anger or electric adrenaline. I was on a boat and it was taking me somewhere and there was nothing I could do but wait. The sun was warm, and the motion of the boat was soothing, and I was suddenly very, very tired.

In the water there were creatures surfacing and diving, over and again. A school of gunmetal-grey fish the size of smallish dogs, each with twisted, cobalt-blue bulls' horns poking out of their heads. Their faces were the blank, impassive faces unique to fish, and their gold eyes were flat, dumb pools.

All, that is, except for the fish with the sewn-up eye.

There it was, The Clackity, and it was smiling at me with its rows of broken razor teeth.

The Clackity fish kept pace with the boat, grinning its mad grin. I whacked at it a few times with an oar, but it was mostly on principle. My heart wasn't in it. I was too exhausted to care if The Clackity knew I was in the boat or not.

I pulled my backpack up on the bench and rested my head on it as I watched the beach recede into the distance. The last thing I saw before I fell asleep was John Jeffrey Pope standing on the shore.

This time I waved.

16

I woke up with a start.

My whole body was on high alert, and Bird's little feet tickled as he marched back and forth across my back.

Something was wrong.

I was thirsty, and definitely sunburned, but that wasn't it.

No, it was the boat. Something had jerked it back, hard enough to pull me out of my sleep. It was no longer moving at its slow, steady pace. The black rowboat was still, bobbing in place halfway between the shore and the island.

My eyes were foggy, and my brain was foggier, and I guess that was why I didn't see the hands at first.

I pushed the sunglasses to the top of my head and squinted at the mean sun. It didn't look as though it had moved at all. Not since the time I'd fallen asleep and maybe, I realized, not since this day had started. It hung right in the middle of the purple sky, same as ever.

The Clackity had said *best before the sun goes down*, but maybe that was another one of his tricks. Maybe the sun never went down here, and this day would go on and on until I either found Des, or . . .

Nope. No *or*.

I would find D, get her home, and be done with this place. I reached for the oars. If the boat wouldn't go on its own, I could take it from here.

It was then that I saw them. I almost touched them— they were so close to the oar handles. Two hands. Two sets of long, pale fingers with long, pale nails, grasping either side of the rowboat.

I made an embarrassing little squeak of a sound and fell off the bench into the back of the boat. My butt was hurt, and so was my pride, but I was scared enough not to care about either very much. I didn't blink as the hand on the right disappeared and then joined the hand on the left. The owner of the hands pulled herself up and into the boat. It rocked enough that I thought it might tip, and the idea of falling into the dark water scared me as much as the thing climbing in to join me.

As soon as she was in the rowboat, it began moving again. But slower this time. As if it was no longer sure it wanted to take us to the island after all.

She was drenched, her moss-colored hair hanging all down the front of her face like a mask. Or a shroud. All that lank hair in her face made her look like something out of a scary movie, like maybe she didn't even have a face underneath.

She sat down on the second bench, her hidden face turned toward me. I couldn't see her eyes, but I could feel them. And like a small animal that's been spotted by a much larger predator, I was frozen.

For what felt like forever she just sat, hunched over

and motionless. Then her hands moved up from the bench and I scooted back as far as I could, which wasn't very far at all. But she didn't lurch or grab for me with her talon fingers. Instead she reached up and pushed her hair out of her face. Before her hands were all the way through her knotted hair, it was completely dry. And so was the rest of her. I could see her clearly then, and I knew immediately who was in the boat with me.

The knowing didn't make me feel a bit better.

She had wide eyes, a pointed chin, and thick, arched eyebrows. She had a dark mole on her left cheekbone. She was green all over, from her too-pale-looking skin to her nearly black hair. And her eyes were sickly emeralds. The fine crinkles around them were the only indication that she was older than Grey, Gold, and Pink.

This, I knew, was their mother.

"Did the worthless ghouls give you a key?" Her voice was flat, but her pale hands were angry as they clutched her green calico dress in tight fists.

It took me a minute to understand. Then I was mad. Being mad didn't stop my heart from trying to escape my rib cage, but it did unfreeze me a little. I needed to remember that trick.

"The penny-eyed ghosts? Yes. And they aren't ghouls, and they aren't worthless. They were very nice to me."

"And before that? Who gave you a key before that? Was it my worthless pink daughter? She was always the dumbest of a stupid litter."

I went from mad straight to livid.

"Pink isn't worthless *or* dumb. She's sweet and . . . and a very good artist. Besides, she didn't give me the key. Grey did."

"Nonsense," Mother Witch hissed. "She would have eaten you without bothering to cook you first."

"They're going vegetarian," I informed her.

I watched, fascinated, as shame and sorrow and rage traded places on the green woman's face. "*Vegetarian.* I'm glad to be done with them, awful little trio of creatures. No mother deserves such disappointment." Her self-pity was disgusting.

I said the first thing that came to mind. In hindsight, it wasn't very smart. I was in a small boat with a witch so mean even Grey seemed afraid of her. But I said it anyway. "I think you should leave."

Mother Witch laughed a fingernails-on-a-chalkboard

laugh. "I think I'll stay. I've been waiting for this boat a very long time."

"In the lake?"

"Of course in the lake, twit." She was definitely Grey's mother. "The boat is the only way to the island. Without it, you can swim and swim and never get any closer than when you started. I've been swimming for longer than you've been alive."

A fierce spark of hope lit in my stomach. Maybe that meant Pope couldn't . . .

"Unless you're a ghoul. The rules are different for the dead ones."

The little spark was extinguished, pinched out by her words.

She held out one wicked hand. "Give me the key."

Bird beat his wings on my back in a panicked flurry, but he didn't have to tell me that giving the key to Mother Witch was a terrible idea.

"No."

She sighed. When she spoke next, she sounded bored. "Give me the key or I will eat you and throw your bones into the lake for the creatures at the bottom to sharpen their teeth on."

"No."

She leaned forward and looked at me for a while. She was squinting—reading me, trying to learn something. When she did, she smiled. Her teeth were white against her dark mouth. It was not a very nice smile. "Give me the key, or I will go back for your ghouls. And then I will go back for my girls. And then I will find whoever it is you're looking for. But first, your bones will go into the lake."

I didn't know whether she could do all the things she said she would, but I believed she would try.

Bird fluttered in a way that told me he was scared, and his being scared made me more than slightly petrified.

Maybe I didn't have a choice.

I started to reach for my little collection of keys but stopped with my hand at the very edge of my pocket. She was still squinting in my direction, but her eyes didn't follow my hand as it moved.

So I lifted my hand and waved at her, wiggling my sweaty fingers.

Her expression didn't change.

I waved bigger, a dramatic, parade-float-princess kind of wave.

Nothing.

She couldn't see.

Maybe because she didn't have her glasses, lost somewhere at the bottom of the black lake. Or maybe she was old enough to have gone totally blind, as witches do. But I was absolutely certain that she couldn't see me well enough for it to mean anything at all. I was also certain I couldn't let her know I knew.

I thought as fast as I could. I was only a step or two ahead of myself, hoping what I was about to do would work. If I could get to the island, maybe I could lose her.

"Okay," I said. "I'll get you the key."

I grabbed my backpack and pulled Aunt D's purse from it. I dug around the bottom of the purse until I found the spare house key. It was brass, with KwicKey stamped at the top, just like almost every key to every house in the world. I'd been with Des when she had it printed at the hardware store.

If Mother Witch could see at all, if I was wrong, she'd know in a second this wasn't the key she wanted.

I held it out to her. "Here. Here's your key. Just don't hurt them."

She didn't move to take it. Instead she held out her own hand. "Don't be impudent. Give me the key like a good girl."

"How do I know you won't eat me after I give it to you?"

"Because you stink. You'd be sour and curdled."

I was a little defensive. "Well, it's been a long day and I haven't exactly had time for a bath."

She leaned forward, closer, and sniffed the air around me. It made me very uncomfortable. "You smell marked. Nasty."

Marked. *Nasty.* It was the same word The Clackity had used when Bird burned himself onto my shoulder. She couldn't see Bird, but she could smell him. I reached back and patted him gently, hoping he understood my *thank you.*

His puffed-up chest told me he did and was proud of himself.

"Besides," she continued, "you might be useful once we reach the island. Now, the key."

I dropped the house key into her outstretched hand and pulled away quickly before she could change her mind. She ran her pointed fingers over the wrong key, feeling its bumps and ridges. She sniffed at it and grimaced. "It stinks like you, but no matter. A lock doesn't care what a key smells like. Most locks, anyway." She dropped the key into a pocket of her green dress and sat back, relaxed now that she had what she wanted.

The rest of the boat ride was quiet. I didn't see the Clackity fish again, or any other fish for that matter. They didn't want to be with Mother Witch any more than I did.

We drew near the island, and I got a good look at it for the first time. Beyond the rocky, shallow shore was a dense forest, and these trees looked like proper trees. I didn't see any sign of life, but that didn't mean nothing lived there.

The boat pulled itself onto grey, stony sand, nothing like the pyrite sand of the desert I'd crossed. The oars did a little flip and dug themselves into the beach, anchoring the rowboat in place. I wondered if the rowboat would eventually take itself back across the lake after it made itself a new key from sticks and leaves in the forest.

I stood, grabbed my backpack, and jumped out of the boat. I was anxious to put some space between me and Mother Witch. When I glanced back, she was gone. When I turned away and toward the forest, she was there, standing between me and the tree line. She was so close I nearly ran into her. Holy heck, she was fast.

Witches, I decided, were frustrating.

"Well," I said, "thanks for not eating me."

"We're not finished, girl. And don't mistake my reluctance to eat you for refusal. You'll spend a few more minutes helping me, I think."

"Helping you what?"

"Helping me find the house, of course. And, probably, killing the man who lives there. But I'll not be eating that one. He's poison."

I didn't want to go with Mother Witch, but I didn't think I had much of a choice. Besides, I figured she might know at least a little about the fifth house, and that would be useful. I reached back and tapped Bird, hoping he'd share his opinion of the situation, but I could feel he was distracted by something behind us.

I looked back just in time to see the Clackity fish writhe its way out of the lake. It beached itself, flopping around like, well, a fish out of water.

I felt a pang of sympathy for the fish—not the Clackity part, but for what it had been before Clackity stole it from itself. I started toward the fish, meaning to throw it back in the black lake to be with its friends. I would let Bird do his work again, sending Clackity out of the fish like he had done for the penny-eyed ghost and the little fawn.

I grabbed it around the middle, or as close to the middle as I could get with all the flopping and fighting it was doing.

Mother Witch, who probably couldn't see well enough

to know what I was up to, bellowed, "Girl! You're in no position to waste my time!"

I started to answer her, but instead I yelled out, surprised when my hands began to burn, and dropped the Clackity fish as fast as I'd picked it up. Too fast, even, for Bird to run The Clackity out.

The Clackity fish wasn't slippery or slimy. Picking it up felt like grabbing a heavy, wet cactus. It stung my hands with a hundred tiny needles. They were so small I couldn't see them, but I *felt* them for sure. My hands were on fire.

I said a bunch of words that would have gotten me grounded for a month.

The Clackity fish grinned at me even as it fell back to the beach with a thick thud. Its grin said, *See what I can do even when I'm not really there? Remember to be afraid, Pretty Penny.*

I was hurt, but I was angry, too. And scared.

My heart pounded in my ears and I waved my hands around in the air, trying to get the burning to stop. I reared back to kick the Clackity fish into the lake like a soccer ball. But I stopped my kick mid-swing when the Clackity fish started vibrating. It was having some sort of a fit, a seizure.

I backpedaled fast. I didn't know whether it was about to attack or explode, but it was doing *something*. Whatever was about to happen, I didn't want to be anywhere near it when it did.

Then it froze, and eight spindly spider's legs poked

through its scales, wriggling and scritching around for dry land. As it pulled itself up, its tail fell off, dragged itself back into the lake, and disappeared. It was so weird, so alien, I couldn't even be scared of it. My eyes must have bugged out like a cartoon character's. Between that and all my swearing and hand waving, I was sure I looked ridiculous, but honestly I didn't care. The only other person there was Mother Witch, and she was mostly blind, anyway.

Six new eyes popped open on the Clackity thing's face, and it became a Clackity sort-of-spider. The Clackity gave me a familiar toothy smile—that part never changed—winked its seven good eyes, and scuttled *click click click* into the forest. I lost sight of it in the brambles and branches and shadows.

My hands stopped burning even before The Clackity disappeared, but the memory of the pain remained a fresh warning that I wouldn't soon forget. It was the first time The Clackity had hurt me, and I didn't have any reason to believe it would be the last.

Clackity could harm me and wanted me to know it didn't mind doing it. When that idea settled in my brain, I got truly scared, because there was still a long way to go and Clackity wasn't playing by any rules, as far as I could tell.

Maybe this wasn't a quest after all.

Maybe it was *survival*, and that changed everything.

My whole body tensed up, and I probably would have stood right there on the beach until the tide took me away if Mother Witch hadn't interrupted my freak-out.

"You failed to tell me you brought that creature with you," Mother Witch said, and made a face like she'd smelled something gross. "I might have waited for another day if I'd known your friend was back. It's mad and makes things more complicated than they need be. Let's move on before it decides it wants to play with us."

Mother Witch took me by the arm, and with a yank she unglued my feet from where they were stuck to the ground. My whole body wanted to pull away from her touch, but I didn't. As awful as she was, someone was telling me where to go and what to do, and in a really messed-up way, it was a relief.

She wasn't being friendly by taking my arm. She needed me to keep her from tripping and falling as we made our way into the dense, shadowy woods. I took a deep breath and held it, because this forest smelled like it was supposed to—dirt and bark and green things. It smelled so normal I was homesick all over again.

"It's not my friend, and I didn't bring it here. It sent me because of my aunt, and because of John Jeffrey Pope." I didn't feel like explaining it to her, but it turned out I didn't have to.

"Ah. That explains that. It likes games, and it likes to win its games. Don't think it'll play fair, though, girl, even if it made a bargain with you. It won't cheat, not outright, but it will . . . interpret . . . the rules. And you'll be wise to remember it's the one who made those rules."

My head had cleared enough for me to get suspicious. "Why are you being helpful?"

Mother Witch grabbed the tops of my bare arms in

her pointed fingers. They dug in, and her nails were like claws. My eyes watered with surprise and pain. As a tear ran down my face, Mother Witch let go with one hand and swiped it off my cheek. My tear stood on her finger-tip like a dewdrop and then grew until it was the size of a grape. She studied it for a moment, then popped my tear into her mouth.

It must not have tasted very good, because Mother Witch grimaced. "I don't have much use for you, but I detest that broken ghoul. I'll likely eat you even though you taste spoiled and sour. If I don't, I hope you best it at its game."

"Do you know how to beat it?" My voice came out a whisper and shook as I asked. I needed to get her off the topic of eating me and back to The Clackity.

"Of course not. I'd never be fool enough to enter an arrangement with it. But it seems we have a common enemy, and a common goal. So, perhaps"—she seemed noncommittal about it—"we'll find the next house together."

I thought about this. "Why do you want to kill the man who lives there?"

"Because he's as bad and mad as The Clackity. And because he's stolen my stories and I want them back."

"How can someone steal stories?"

Keep her thinking about stories and not about eating me.

"The usual way. He climbs through your window at night while you sleep and steals them from your head." Mother Witch twisted her fingers around in the air like she was gathering dust motes or cobwebs. "He reaches in and plucks them out. It doesn't hurt—unless you're awake—and then it feels like someone is tearing tiny holes in your mind and pulling earwigs and centipedes out of it. Very unpleasant."

Mother Witch began to pinch my arm, checking the meat on my bones.

"Did he steal all your stories?" None of this made a lot of sense, but I wanted Mother Witch to keep talking, and to stop her meal planning with me as the main course. If I was going to run for it, I first wanted to learn as much as I could about what was waiting for me in the fifth house.

I took a half step backward, hoping the whole time she wouldn't notice.

"Of course not, twit. I have many, many stories. I am too old and too full of tales for him to ever take them all. But he took some I loved very much, and those stories bit and stung as they went. I was their home, and they didn't want to go." Mother Witch's eyes were sad.

Heat crawled up my neck and into my cheeks. I was angry that she didn't miss her daughters but missed her stupid stories.

"I think I understand."

"I doubt it," Mother Witch answered me. "You don't taste very smart to me, but it's not as though I can be picky."

Her taste buds are as bad as her eyesight, I thought as I pressed on with my next question. "What will you do when you get your stories back?"

I took another half step, inch by inch getting out of reach of her mean fingers.

"I'll hope they remember me and crawl back into their nest, of course."

I managed another half step.

Then another.

I was about to run when her hand came crashing down on my wrist like a police cuff.

"Hmph," she said. "I may be nearly blind, but I am older and wiser than you could hope to be in a half-hundred lifetimes. I can smell a meal trying to escape."

It wasn't a stretch of the imagination to believe she was envisioning me being served alongside her pink daughter's herb-butter-slathered bread. Her eyes were hungry.

I had one card left to play. I'd been holding it for just the right time. I hoped I hadn't waited too long, that the chance to use it hadn't passed.

I took as deep a breath as I could, but my voice still shook. "I have something for you. Something your grey daughter sent with me. She thought I might meet you, and I did, so now you can have it."

A look of surprise crossed her face, and Mother Witch tilted her head in thought. "As I said, she was the best of a bad litter. I'm not surprised she sent something when the other two were too thoughtless to do the same."

Knowing she couldn't see me, I rolled my eyes. She really was the worst. "I have to find it. It's in my back-pack."

Her blind eyes narrowed, but I could see the greed in

them. She wanted her present. "If this is a trick, I won't stop with your tears."

"I promise. I really do have a gift for you."

Mother Witch released my wrist, leaving angry red welts behind.

I didn't have to look hard for Grey's gift. The paper bag was at the very top of my backpack, as I wanted to be sure not to crush the flower within. It made a rattling, crinkling noise in my shaking hands. Mother Witch might not be able to see how nervous I was, but she would definitely be able to hear it.

She held her hand out expectantly. When the paper sack touched her palm, she snatched it away from me and reached in with her fish-belly-pale fingers. As I wiped my hands on my jeans for the thousandth time that day, she pulled the gold, grey, and pink flower out of the bag and ran her fingers over it, feeling the leaves and petals and stem.

I don't know what I expected her reaction to be, but a growing look of terror wasn't it at all.

She reached her hand out faster than I could have imagined possible, even for a witch, and latched onto my right arm. Her voice was thick with fear as she asked, "What color is this thing?"

"Gold stem, grey petals, and a pink middle," I told her, trying to pull myself out of her grasp as I spoke. "I thought you'd like it. It was special, the only one Grey had in the pot, and it's really pretty. . . ." I stopped my nervous stammering because I could no longer hear myself over the high-pitched keening coming from Mother Witch.

She tried to drop the flower, but it refused to fall. Somehow, the flower had stuck itself to her hand.

Then I saw that was wrong; it hadn't *stuck* itself. The fine stem had grown—*burrowed*—into the center of her palm. Delicate gold vines began to grow out of her wrist, and then her arm, and from those vines gold leaves and tiny grey flower buds appeared.

The flowered vines grew across her shoulders and her arms. They grew up into her lank, dark hair, making a kind of veil and then a crown. Soon she was covered in tightly wound vines. They crawled down her legs and to the ground, then they dug into the soil and continued to move as they made their way deeper and deeper into the forest floor.

And then it got stranger.

Her smooth green skin began to brown in patches as it turned rough and hard. Her legs twisted together as her feet disappeared into the dirt. The hand she held me with became branches and sticks, and still she didn't let me go. She gripped me tight as she began to grow taller and taller, and I stopped breathing as we rose into the air.

At twenty, then thirty feet, she was still wailing. I was high in the air. Way too high. As we rose, I caught a glimpse of the beach from between the trees. All the other trees surrounding us stayed right where they belonged. In fact, it felt like the whole forest had grown still and watchful, and we were the only things moving at all.

At fifty, then sixty feet, she was cursing me and her daughters and everyone we loved. I wanted to close my eyes so I wouldn't have to look down, but they refused to cooperate.

By eighty feet, she was only humming, her words muffled because she could no longer open her mouth. I couldn't see much anymore through my tears. My heart had dropped out of its usual spot in my throat, straight down to my feet.

At maybe one hundred feet, we stopped. I was hyperventilating. The only thing between me and certain death were the branches and twigs that had been her hand just a minute before.

Her face was gone then, and all that remained were the vague impressions of where her eyes would have been. Her bark and branches were caramel brown, covered in gold leaves and vines with grey and pink flowers. Even as I struggled to breathe and my feet sweated through my socks, it registered somewhere in the back of my brain that she was beautiful.

I hung there among her new leaves, my feet kicking and finding nothing but more open air, until, somehow, they found a foothold on a strong branch below. Slowly, I untangled from what used to be green fingers and steadied myself. The whole time, I was making a sound that was part moan, part whine, and 100 percent terror. Heights, in my estimation, were a million times worse than witches, and I was shaking so hard I thought I'd launch myself to the ground.

My hands were wet with sweat, slippery on the branch above me as I clung to it quite literally for dear life. I felt Bird move to the middle of my back, maybe to help center

LORA SENF

me, and then he was as still as I'd ever felt him. He didn't beat his wings or even flutter, but I heard that small voice. *One step. Just take one step. Then one more.*

Another voice in my head, mine this time, said, *Focus. Breathe. Focus. Breathe*, over and over and over again.

I moved so slowly a snail would have passed me. I took one shaking step at a time toward the trunk, where I could cling to it and think of a way to get myself down without dying. As I neared the center, the whole situation changed and became stranger still.

Where her heart would have been, there was a hole in the trunk of the now-tree that used to be Mother Witch. It was a very small hole, just the right size for a key made from twigs. And then, because now I was looking for it, I found the faintest outline of a small, arched door.

Mother Witch had become the fifth house.

18

I tried to convince my right hand to let go of the branch above so it could fumble around in my pocket for the twig-and-leaf key. It is a small thing, moving your hand from one place to another, but in that moment it was impossible. The longer I hung there, the more I panicked, and the more I shook, the more impossible it all became. The new tree was done growing and the ground didn't recede, but it seemed farther and farther away, and I became certain I was going to die in the next moment, or the moment after that.

I closed my eyes, not wanting to see the Mother Witch tree or the ground below me or the empty air all around. I took shallow breaths I wished were deep and willed the panic to pass.

No one was coming to save me while I tried my best to save Aunt Des.

That was the first time in the whole of the day that I thought I really might fail; the first time I knew failure was not only possible but likely. And as soon as I realized that, the idea was like a foghorn in my brain. It was everywhere and constant and I couldn't get away from it.

I might fail.

I will fail.

If Bird hadn't moved then, it might have been the end.

But Bird did move. He crept slowly, softly, up my back and across my shoulder. He was gentle, and the almost nothingness of him did not throw me off-balance. He crept up my right arm to my hand, and then he was in my palm, between it and the branch. With Bird in my hand, it became lighter and surer in the empty air all around us. It let go of the branch and drifted down, and I had never been as graceful as I was right then. I probably never will be again. My hand belonged to an airborne ballerina as it reached into my pocket and pulled out the twig-and-leaf key. No fumbling—my hand chose the right key the first time.

The calm in my hand spread through my whole body, and my panic was gone like it had never been anything but someone else's idea. I wasn't shaking anymore as I slid the key into the place where Mother Witch's heart had been. It turned with the sound of a million autumn leaves rustling in a campfire breeze.

I don't know whether I said it out loud or just thought it very loudly, but I asked Bird, "How did you do that?"

I didn't. You did.

I didn't believe him, but it didn't matter. I could think and breathe and that was enough.

A light as black as the sun in the purple sky shone through the cracks between the Mother Witch tree and the little arched door. The door swung open and the rustling leaf sound was gone. All the sounds in the forest were gone, even the sounds so small and natural you don't hear them until they go missing.

The sight beyond the door was as black as the woods were quiet. I didn't want to go through that door and into the shifting nothing. The same nothing I'd almost leapt into in the silhouette neighborhood.

This time Bird didn't peck me, telling me *Stop! Do not go there!* Instead he returned to my shoulder, where he beat his wings, gentle and insistent, and what he was saying was, *You need to go in now. Because this will never get any better.*

The door was short, maybe four feet tall. I crouched down as I lifted one foot from the branch and stepped into the nothing. I couldn't see my foot, or the part of my leg that had crossed the border between the forest and wherever the next place was, but it touched down on something solid.

"You sure, buddy?"

A shrug and a single flap of his wings. *I am. But you have to be too.*

And then I was. Because I didn't have a choice. Nowhere to go but down, and that wasn't really a choice at all.

I plucked one of the grey-and-pink flowers hanging just over my head and dropped it into my open backpack. The first one had been useful, so maybe it was wise to keep one more just in case.

I took a deep breath, stooped low, and crept through the small, arched door. It wasn't hot or cold in Mother

Witch's wooden heart. It didn't smell or sound like any-thing. It was only empty.

I went on like that, crouched over because of my backpack brushing up against a ceiling I couldn't see, for as long as I could. There were no curves or bends in the dark passage, but it did change. It sloped up, only gradu-ally, but enough that I noticed it. And the passage seemed to be getting smaller, shorter.

I had to crouch even lower.

My brain kept trying to tell me I was trapped, and I kept telling it to shut up.

After a while, I couldn't get low enough for my back-pack to clear the top of the passageway, so I started to crawl. In a way, that was better, because my back was starting to hurt. Pretty soon, though, I missed walking even if it meant I was bent nearly in half. Crawling a long distance is harder than it looks.

I would have run face-first into the end of the pas-sage but was saved from a broken nose by a seam of golden light no wider than a thread. The outline of a door emerged in the dark, lit from whatever was on the other side. The door was just like the one I'd come through, arched at the top, only shorter. I felt around it, looking with my fingers for a knob or a latch or a keyhole. There was nothing but rough, unsanded wood. I pushed on it just a bit, testing it. Maybe I should have worried about what would be waiting on the other side, but all I cared about was getting out of that dark and crowded place. The door gave a little, so I pushed harder with both hands, and that time it flew open.

I fell through the door and onto the smooth wooden floor of the fifth house. The air around me was so bright and yellow that I had to shield my eyes, since they'd become accustomed to the black nothing in the passage.

I stood up before my eyes remembered how to see, which was a mistake. I hit my head on the ceiling hard enough to make me swear. I was so focused on trying to, well, focus, that I hadn't noticed Bird's frantic wings beating against my neck. It wasn't until he started pecking at me that I remembered he was there at all.

My time in all the dark nothing had sort of hypnotized me, and my brain was as fuzzy as my eyes.

"Stop it, Bird!" I slapped at the back of my neck.

"Sad, sad." The voice came from my right, as thin and dry as paper. "Pretty enough, but she's no princess, is she? A princess would not be so low as to curse, and she would never strike herself. No, this one is as common a girl as ever there was."

I narrowed my eyes in the direction of the voice. As they adjusted, I could make out a very, very pale form across the room. Then, more clearly, two long arms and two even longer legs. The creature looked like a man in the face and head and torso, but his arms and legs were bent up and back like a grasshopper's, and he stood on all fours. He wore what was left of a tattered shirt and pants, but they were short on him, like maybe his arms and legs hadn't always been quite so long. He came closer and did not walk as much as he skittered across the wooden floor of the room. As he did, smaller, many-legged creatures dodged his hands and feet. Not all of them moved in time, and there was a light crunch every time one of the insects was crushed.

The room, I saw then, was bright yellow because the black sunlight streamed through a pair of pale green windows and reflected off the pages of open books and piles of gold coins. The room was full of both. The floor and ceiling and walls were all made of the same light wood, which made sense, since we were somewhere deep in the Mother Witch tree. Along the walls and in the corners and throughout the piles of books and treasure, more insects squirmed and scuttled.

In the center of the room was a rough-hewn wooden

table, and on the table was a burlap sack. I considered how far I'd climbed, and how full the room was of hoarded books and treasure. And I considered those two green windows. Green like Mother Witch's eyes.

I didn't like it, but I thought I understood. "Are we in her head?"

The pale creature smiled, and I saw that all his teeth were gone. "Of course we are. She was full of so many stories, even after I stole her oldest and her favorites. I would take a story, and she would replace it with two new ones. She was a grand spinner of tales, and while I'm pleased to be here now, I am sorry she will never make me another."

So this was the Story Thief.

"She was looking for you, you know. How long have you been in here, in her head?"

He reached a spindly arm back so he could scratch his chin in thought. "Oh, I've been here since she grew and grew and became this house. Maybe many long years, maybe a few minutes. I can't be sure, as I lost track of time before she was born. So I don't suppose it matters much, does it?"

I was tired and my back ached from crawling through the tunnel. And I was worried about my aunt. But more than anything, I was absolutely, sincerely done with strange people who talked in riddles.

"I need a key. Please." I tacked on the *please* just in case he cared about manners. But he already thought I was common, so it probably didn't make much difference.

The Story Thief skittered a little closer and pushed

his face toward me, staring with ink-pool eyes. He cocked his head so far on his long neck it nearly went upside down. "You *do* need a key. A key for the next chapter. A key to finish your story."

"Yes, I . . ."

"All stories are keys, you know." The Story Thief's dark eyes seemed to get bigger, and I found I couldn't look away from them. They were as deep as the nothingness had been. Softly, he continued, "All stories are keys to a truth. Sometimes a truth about the world. Sometimes a truth about love or fear. Sometimes, even, a truth about a lie. But all keys, all truths."

I nodded, agreeing with him even if I wasn't entirely sure what he meant. It was his eyes, I think, that did it. I was a housefly under the hypnotic spell of a spider.

"So, tell me a story, girl. Tell me an important truth."

Without thinking, I began, "When I was little, my house burned down and my parents . . ."

I paused. I thought maybe I didn't want to tell him this story at all.

But as soon as the thought came it was gone. I was so lost in those endless eyes, I couldn't remember what I'd been worried about just a moment before. So I continued, "I . . . I was little. And away for the night at a friend's house. And while I was gone, there was a fire . . . and . . . Stop it!"

I was yanked out of the trance by the feeling of something in my hair. It could have been a bug—a big one— or it could have been the Story Thief's fingers. He jerked away too quickly for me to be sure.

A look of disappointment—and maybe anger—crossed the creature's face, but his eyes were back to their regular size. And, more importantly, I could think straight again.

"What were you doing to me? Were you going to steal a story from me? A story about my *parents*?" I was livid. "I can't believe—"

The Story Thief interrupted as he rushed past me to put his ear against the now-closed door I'd just come through. The breeze he stirred up smelled like mildewed parchment.

"Girl," he whispered loudly, "your story has more than one ending. There is a man just now climbing into the same door you unlocked, and perhaps he can finish your story in this room if you want him to be the one to tell it."

Pope. I had to get moving. "No, that is *not* how my story ends."

"Not for you to decide!" the Story Thief barked as he went to the table in the center of the room. From inside the burlap sack he pulled out a random assortment of objects and caressed each one like it was treasure. He laid them out carefully on the table's surface.

As I watched, I found I recognized them. More importantly, I recognized the stories they belonged to.

"I have no key for you, but I will give you a gift. Choose one of these, girl, and it is yours." He waved his hands over the items, displaying them proudly for me.

"I don't want any of those. I want a key."

"None of my keys unlock your story! They each already have a story, and none of them are yours. Now, choose! It is rude to decline a gift from a giver."

"I don't want your gifts. They're all tricks."

The Story Thief was a bad actor, and the look of offended surprise he gave me was not convincing. "I don't know what you mean," he lied.

I was angry and impatient and running out of time. "Yes, you do. You know exactly what these are."

I walked to the left side of the table and pointed at the first object. "This apple. It's bright red. It's perfect, and you know it's poison. Everyone knows 'Snow White.'"

"Perhaps. What of this?" He pointed to a tiny spinning wheel.

"I'll prick my finger on it and fall asleep at the very least. Maybe die. It's 'Sleeping Beauty.' Come on."

"This, then!" He was enjoying himself.

"A mirror? Are you kidding? As if there has ever been a good mirror in any story ever. They're always evil, or cursed, or they lie. No, thank you."

The Story Thief nodded, impressed. "These, then."

I looked at the last of the small collection on the table: a pair of scarlet-red ballet slippers. They were tempting, soft and beautiful. But I knew better. "Not a chance. These are the very worst. 'The Red Shoes' is one of my favorite stories—my friend Lily read it to me once, and then I made her read it a hundred times more. If I put those on, I'll dance and dance and dance until I die or someone comes by with an axe and cuts my feet off."

The Story Thief nodded. "Well done, girl. You love the stories as well as the old witch did. But it changes nothing. I have no key for you and your tale."

I stepped back from the Story Thief. His mildewed-parchment smell was making me queasy. I closed my eyes and concentrated on what to do next, since he wouldn't help. When the idea came to me, I wasn't sure if it would work. Even if it did, it was going to be—what did Mother Witch call it?—*unpleasant.*

"What if I tell you a story? A story with my key in it? And then you take the story out of my brain and put it in your bag. Then you can keep it all—all except my key."

The Story Thief grinned his toothless grin. "You will *give* me a story? How wonderful. I usually have to take them for myself, you know. Yes, I will trade you a new story for your key. I cannot promise it will work. But either way, I shall have two new stories. The one you tell me and the one we are making now."

I didn't trust him, but what else could I do?

I closed my eyes again and thought about the story. I had to get it just right. I needed a key for a lock I hadn't yet seen. . . .

When I opened my eyes again, I had it. It was the last story in the giant collection of Brothers Grimm fairy tales I'd read at least a hundred times. I only hoped I could remember it properly.

The story I told him went like this:

⟶ *THE GOLDEN KEY* ⟶

Once upon a time, there was a little boy
who was very poor, as poor as his parents,
who were poorer even than their parents

before them. Theirs was a bad luck family, and nothing good other than warm broth and the love of his parents had ever happened to the little boy.

One evening, when the winter days were short and the nights too long, the family ran out of firewood and there was only one blanket between them. So the little boy was sent out on his sled to go to the forest and fetch what wood he could find and carry.

The snow was deep, his pants were short, and the little boy had no shoes. Soon he grew cold and miserable, but as he was accustomed to being too cold, it did not slow him. He went into the black woods and gathered what wood he could find and carry, knowing all the while that most of it was far too wet to burn and the family would have a cold and sleepless night before them.

There were seven pieces of dry wood, so the little boy decided to make a small fire by which to warm himself, knowing that if he did not, he would freeze to death before he reached his home. The child scraped the snow away from the ground as best he could, and under the snow he found a golden key.

The boy was smart, and he knew that when one finds a key there is often a lock somewhere close by. So the little boy dug into the ground with frozen fingers until they brushed against a metal object. When he finally unearthed the thing, he was delighted to see it was a small iron chest.

"Perhaps the key will fit," the little boy said aloud to no one, although there were many ears in the forest to hear him. "Perhaps there is something valuable in the chest, and with it I can make a trade and surprise Mother and Father with potatoes and turnips for our broth." So poor was the boy, he did not know how to dream of butter and meat, as he had never tasted either.

At first he found no keyhole, and that made him cry. But when his tears froze his eyes shut, he knew it was not the time for self-pity. Finally he was able to open his eyes once more, and then he found a keyhole, which had been easy to miss, as it was so small and the woods were so dark.

The little boy said a small prayer as he tried the key.

The prayer was answered, and the key fit.

The little boy turned the key and . . .

And now you and I must wait until the child is done unlocking the chest.

We must wait until he has opened the heavy lid.

Only then, when he has opened the chest, will you and I discover if the little boy found bits of treasure there.

Or if he found something much worse.
Perhaps a gift.
Perhaps a curse.
Until then, I cannot say.
And neither can you.
The End

The Story Thief rocked back and forth on his long limbs. He drummed his long fingers on his chin and thought. Finally he said, "That was not a story. You promised me a story, but all you gave me were a beginning and middle. Every story has an ending."

I shook my head, "My story had an ending. You just didn't like it."

"There was no happily ever after! No moral, even." He crossed his long arms over his chest and turned his head so he didn't have to look at me. The Story Thief was sulking.

"Not every story ends that way. Some stories end in a cliff-hanger. That's what makes you want to read the next one, and the one after that."

The Story Thief nodded grudgingly, not liking that I was right. "And how do you know your key will work? How do you know it will let you into the next house?"

"Because I told the story. And I'll decide what happens in the next one."

I had no idea whether that was really true, but it was the best answer I had.

The Story Thief nodded again. It seemed to make sense to him. "Come, then, girl," he said, motioning toward the table with a long finger.

I did, but I dreaded it. Mother Witch told me it was unpleasant, having stories taken from you while you were awake. My heart sped up as I tried to decide if *unpleasant* would mean uncomfortable, or actually painful.

When I got to the table, the Story Thief placed his dry hands on my dirty, sweaty ones and pressed them, palms down, to the table.

I turned back to the door, expecting Pope to burst through it any time now. "Can we hurry?"

"Do not fidget. Do not distract me. And do not change your mind when it is half-done. A half-taken story is worse than a story taken. A half-taken story will bite and sting trying to get back home. You won't like it at all." The Story Thief's black eyes were impossible to read, but I didn't sense any malice or trickery in them. He just wanted his new story.

I closed my eyes again.

"Eyes open," he ordered. "You should bear witness to your story while it is still yours. Besides, if it gets away, I will need your help finding it."

"Okay," I whispered. I was terrified, the same way I got terrified right before a shot at a doctor's office. I'm pretty sure Bird was hiding his eyes under his wings.

The fingers of the Story Thief's right hand grew even longer. They became so thin the tips disappeared into the air, too sharp and fine and white to see. He placed his fingers on the back of my head, and something pointed and dry pressed against my scalp. There was pressure, but no pain at all. Then, a pulling sensation.

Something with too many legs wriggled and squirmed as the Story Thief stole my story.

Not really stealing, I thought, *I'm giving it to him. Making a trade. Making a good, fair deal.*

Imagine a long bug being pulled out of your head, but it doesn't want to go, so it fights and kicks on the way out, its tiny little insect feet scuttling on your scalp the entire time. That was what it felt like when the Story Thief used his needle fingers to take my story. It was, in fact, unpleasant.

Throughout it all, Bird didn't move a feather.

There was a soft *pop,* then the wriggling stopped and there was an itchy spot on the back of my head. I reached up to scratch it, and a tiny smear of blood came away on my finger. Less blood than from a paper cut, which, in a way, was what had just happened.

The Story Thief was grinning his empty grin. Pinched between his fingers was a golden centipede. It writhed and twisted in the air, put out about being pulled so rudely from its home. "This is a pretty one," he said happily. "A bit thin, but that is to be expected of a story without a proper ending."

I was too weirded out by the whole thing to argue with him about endings, so I let it go. "Now my key, please?"

The Story Thief nodded as he dropped the centipede into the burlap sack. Then he plunged his long arm into the opening, farther than it should have been able to go into that bag resting on the table. He was in up to his shoulder, bent over the bag and feeling around.

"Ah, here it is!" He pulled his arm out, and in his hand was a golden key, exactly like I imagined the key in my story would look like.

Or at least that was how it seemed. I found I couldn't remember my story very well anymore.

The Story Thief placed the key on the table, and as he did, there was a commotion on the other side of the door I'd come through a few minutes earlier.

Pope. I snatched the key from the table.

It was only then that I realized I didn't see a second door. There was no other way out of the room. "I have to go," I said. "How do I leave?"

"Down the stairs, of course."

"What stairs? There *aren't* any stairs!" Pope was coming sooner or later, and now I had to get to the next house using stairs that didn't exist. I was getting frantic.

"There are always stairs. I bring them with me everywhere for just such an occasion." The Story Thief pulled the burlap bag open. Then he stretched it wider still, wider than it could possibly stretch. Soon the opening of the bag took up most of the table.

I peered into the sack, and sure enough, there was a flight of stairs inside. The top step was just a couple of feet from the opening. Below that, there was a flickering light in the darkness, like a candle in a windowless room.

"I suggest you go." The Story Thief's black eyes were anxious as they turned to the door. "He will be here soon. I'll not make it as easy for him as I did for you. But I don't know that I want any of his stories. They likely carry disease."

"Thank you," I said. "Thank you for helping me."

The Story Thief bowed low. "Thank you, girl, for your story. Not a princess, but not common, either. A fine storyteller is never common."

I climbed up on the table and stepped into the bag. The step below my foot was wooden and felt solid enough. I began to go down the stairs but couldn't see how far they went. When my head was below the opening of the sack, it began to close like it was being pulled by a cord. My stomach tightened a little at being tied up in a sack, even one big enough for stairs.

"Farewell, little storyteller," said the paper-voiced Story Thief. He gave me a toothless smile and wiggled his story-stealing fingers in a wave as the sack drew shut.

The last I saw of him was the worry in his ink-pool eyes.

He cinched the cord tight and the sack closed completely, and I was alone.

19

Well, not entirely alone. Bird was with me, of course. He'd crawled up to peek around my collarbone so he could see what was happening, where we were going.

The staircase was steep and went down and down. The narrow stairs were covered by a once-fancy carpet runner that had seen better days. *Aladdin,* I thought. I wondered how many stories started here and came to my world—or did they get told in my world and make their way here? I wished I'd thought to ask the Story Thief.

The world inside the burlap sack was lit by gas lamps that hung from a grey stone wall. The light they gave was soft and orange. There were shelves on either side of the staircase, short and evenly spaced so that there was a new shelf at eye level every few steps. Each shelf was lined with glass cases and glass boxes and what looked like glass cake platters with rounded glass lids. In each of these was a piece of a story.

In one, a wilting rose.

In another, a small set of drums.

A flute in a long glass box.

A pair of crystal slippers resting on a royal-blue cushion.

A gingerbread house and, next to it, a gingerbread man.

A ball.

A basket.

An axe.

A few of the cases were empty. The objects the Story Thief had quizzed me with—the apple, spinning wheel, mirror, and red shoes—probably belonged in some of them. And I figured some of the cases would be empty until there was a new story to fill them.

It was a museum filled with bits and pieces of all the stories I loved the most. If I hadn't had places to be and things to do (like rescuing Aunt Des from a dead man), I could have stayed there forever.

I was so busy trying to match the collection of items with their stories that I lost track of where I was and stumbled when I reached the bottom of the stairs. When I looked back up, the orange lamplight was gone and the stairway was black.

I turned to face a short stone tunnel. There were no warm lamps to light my way, just a glimpse of the violet sky at the other end. It was enough to see by, but barely. The space was cold and silent, and my footsteps echoed so it sounded like I had company I couldn't see. There was no door at the end of the tunnel.

It didn't so much end as turn into an alleyway.

Back outside, the air was damp and dirty and thick. Paved with cobblestone, the alley was lined with dark stone walls so tall I couldn't see where they ended. The purple sky was a narrow ribbon. There were no doors on those walls, and no windows.

Forward was the only direction I could go, so I did.

At the edges of the walls, rats the size of small cats scurried aimlessly. Grey and brown and hungry-looking, they scattered and scrambled over one another. I found myself wondering what they ate in that barren place, then decided I didn't want to know.

My shoulders were drawn up tight. Even Bird seemed tense, radiating heat like a little patch of sunburn. There was nothing good about the alleyway. It was a place I wanted to be done with as fast as I could. Whatever challenges the next house would put in my way, I figured they had to be better than the rats and endless stone.

I checked the scurrying creatures' faces as best I could. None of them had a sewn-up left eye, and none of them took a special interest in me. If The Clackity was there among the rats, it wasn't letting on.

But I didn't think it was there at all. I had climbed into the heart of the Mother Witch tree and was sure I hadn't been followed. Other than by Pope, of course.

In a weird way, I was sorry The Clackity wasn't hiding in one of the rats. I didn't want Bird to send The Clackity away again—I wanted to stomp on it. The Clackity wasn't playing fair, and next time I wouldn't either.

The sixth house came into view a long time before I reached it.

The cobblestone path led to another staircase, and the sixth house was at the bottom of those stairs, so I

saw its spires first. They were pointed and black. I imagined any bird brave enough to perch on them would be
immediately impaled. It was not a place for birds, and
as I went down the stone stairs, I saw it was not a place
for *anyone*.

Even the rats didn't follow me down.

The sixth house was massive. The biggest house I'd
ever seen by a long shot, it was made of black iron and
decorated, if you could call it that, with every monster I'd
ever read about and some I'd never even dreamed of. The
creatures grew out of the house's walls.

Except that wasn't quite right.

They weren't growing there.

No, they were trying to escape.

The iron monsters moved slowly, but they moved. A
snake with a head like a jackrabbit squirmed in the grasp
of a giant housefly. A spider with horse's legs struggled
to free itself from the wall like it was stuck in quicksand,
while a crocodile with moth's wings tried to escape its
web. Devils and imps and trolls danced and fought and
scurried where the house touched the ground.

None of the nightmare things took any notice of me,
not even when I climbed the many stairs to the sprawling
veranda that lined the front of the house. And none of the
creatures, I noticed, went anywhere near the front door.

I very badly did not want to go through that door,
but there was no way to get around the house even if I
decided I wanted to try to cheat and skip it entirely. The
walls of the alleyway opened up around the sixth house,
but there were only inches between them. The gap was

big enough for Bird to get through, and maybe some of the smaller rats, but it was far too narrow for me.

There were always choices, and I had three.

(a) I could sit on the cobblestones and wait for Pope to find me.

And probably die.

Or (b) I could backtrack up the stairs through the fairy-tale museum, where I would eventually run into Pope.

And probably die.

Or (c) I could go through the iron door of the sixth house.

And *maybe* die.

Since *maybe* was slightly less terrifying than *probably*, the door it was.

The closer I got to the house, the colder I felt. The shadows the building created blocked out the black sun, and I had the very distinct thought that nothing living had any business in those shadows, that close to the house.

In the tale I had told the Story Thief, a golden key opened up an iron chest. My golden key opened the entrance to the iron house like I had known it would. The door squealed and screamed as it swung inward.

At the same time, the creatures trapped in the walls went into a frenzy. They shrieked and howled with rusted iron voices. I didn't know if they were trying to warn me not to go in, or if they wanted to punish me for trying. Either way, the sounds made my heart race and my skin crawl. The golden key nearly slipped out of my wet, shaking hands as I put it back into my pocket.

Because Pope couldn't seem to open any door I closed, and because I didn't want to hear the things in the walls any longer than I had to, I tried to close the door to the sixth house behind me. It wouldn't budge, not even a little.

I pushed so hard, blood pounded like drums in my head.

It didn't move.

I was wasting time.

I gave up on the door and turned to investigate the house. I saw that I was in an enormous ballroom, except in place of a dance floor there was something else. . . .

The inside walls were made of the same black iron as the outside, and they rose dozens of feet in the air, meeting in a dome at the top. In those walls were the back ends of the creatures I'd seen from the front. They pushed and scrambled with their legs and wings and arms, trying to get free.

The whole thing felt like being in an egg, a terrible and poisonous iron egg, filled with creatures who couldn't quite manage to hatch. Part of me wanted to find a way to set all of them free. But the smarter part of me, the part that didn't trust anything about this place, knew that was probably a terrible idea. The things in the walls were as likely to eat me as thank me.

Purple sky and black sun peeked in through narrow windows that ran from the floor to the top of the dome. Between the windows were sconces with candles as tall as me. The candles were the same color as the walls, and the black flames that burned steadily cast the same light as the sun outside.

The room was dim, but there was enough light for me to see what was waiting for me.

And I really, truly almost quit right then and there. If it hadn't been for Des, I would have. Because Aunt D was the only thing in the world I cared about enough to face what was in the middle of the sixth house.

In the center of that room, just feet from the front door, was an abyss. The pit stretched nearly to the edges of the great room, leaving too narrow a ledge to even think about walking on. But there *was* a way to get from one side of the room to the other.

A wooden bridge spanned the pit—two feet wide at the most, and those were the planks that weren't broken off on the ends. There were no rails, not even ropes along the sides.

My only way through the sixth house was across the bridge, over a pit that had no bottom as far as I could tell. A pit that was filled with the dark, swirling nothing I seemed to keep running into.

The only thing that scared me more than heights was the idea of losing Aunt Des forever. But this, the bridge and the pit below it, was something different than heights.

This wasn't falling and eventually landing. Falling into the abyss meant falling forever.

I don't know how I knew it, but I did. And I was more afraid than I'd ever been in my whole life. My hands were sweating, and so were my feet. But my skin was cold. It was cold inside the sixth house, and it was cold inside me, too.

I knelt by the edge of the abyss and looked over as

far as I dared. I guess I was hoping to find another way, something other than that slender thread of a bridge. Maybe another set of stairs. Or a trail like the one that wraps around the inside of the Grand Canyon.

Or . . . anything. Anything but the bridge.

Below, there was nothing but the black nothing.

Everything in me said not to cross the bridge. Everything in me knew I had to.

A tuneless whistling came drifting into the room through the open front door from the alleyway. The whistling could belong to only one person, a person with sandy hair who sauntered with his hands in his pockets. Pope was close.

I moved away from the precipice and stood. I put my pack on and tightened the straps as much as I could. I wasn't going to risk it throwing me off-balance. Just before stepping onto the bridge, I patted Bird gently. He was on my shoulder, still and quiet.

"Buddy, can you move to the middle? You know, for balance."

I felt his shadow self move to the center of my back.

"You ready?"

One strong, sure beat of his wings. *Yes. You can do this. Be calm. Be brave.*

I took a step onto the bridge, certain it would sway under my foot. It didn't. It was steady and sure.

I took another step.

Then another.

My ankles shook and my knees were loose and with every step I was sure they'd give out.

My thoughts began to churn in my head as I did my best to focus on placing one foot in front of the other, not looking ahead or down or anywhere but at my feet, making slow progress.

Too slow, I thought. *Pope won't be this slow. He'll be braver. Faster. Because he can. Because he can't die. Because he's already dead and ghosts don't have to worry about keeping their balance or about their sweaty feet or their backpacks or their aunts.*

My thoughts moved faster and faster, and so did my heart and so did my breath.

The black got blacker and the abyss got deeper, and that might have all been in my head, but it didn't matter because I was done.

I wasn't going to make it.

The panic came on worse than it had since Mom and Dad disappeared. My legs and arms shook and soon my whole body was vibrating. I started making a sound that came from the top of my throat, a whining and wailing kind of sound.

I was frozen, maybe a third of the way across the bridge. My thoughts didn't churn anymore because I couldn't think. I was made of panic and that was all. I couldn't think, and I couldn't hear, either. And if Bird tried to warn me, I didn't feel him.

Two strong hands shoved my back.

I stumbled forward and looked over my shoulder at the same time.

A smiling Pope stood confident as anything on the bridge just behind me.

My left foot went off the side of the bridge where one of the broken boards was especially short. And then the rest of my body twisted and followed.

And then I fell.

I fell into the pit.

I fell.

In my dreams, I fall all the time. I never know why, or what I'm falling from. I just fall and fall while the sky gets bigger and farther away. But those are dreams, and I always wake up in a tangle of sweaty sheets.

This wasn't a dream, or even a nightmare, and I wasn't going to save myself by waking up.

As I fell, I managed to reach up with my right hand and grab at the very edge of the bridge. I couldn't get ahold of it, but I was close enough that I scraped my sweaty fingers on the broken boards.

The falling was fast, and straight down. Just like it was in my dreams.

John Jeffrey Pope stood directly above me on the bridge.

So The Clackity had lied again. I wasn't safe in the houses at all.

Pope watched me as I dropped like a rock, down and down and down. His face was hidden in shadows, but I knew he was smiling.

Then I had fallen too far to see him anymore.

I'd lost.

He'd get to the next house and to Des and there was nothing I could do to stop him. There was nothing I could do but fall.

I fell.

A scream started in my stomach and made its way to my chest. It burned when it came up my throat, and by the time it escaped my mouth it was full of terror and rage, but mostly it was made of heartbreak.

I fell.

I'd gotten so close, so close to being the hero of my own story, and my stupid panic had finally done the one thing I swore I'd never let it do. It had stopped me, and it had won.

I fell.

I inhaled to feed another scream but gasped instead. Bird moved on my back, except it wasn't his usual little flits and rustles. It was bigger and stronger than before. *He* was bigger and stronger.

Bird stretched and grew and soon his silhouette wings were too big for my back. They grew past my ribs and over my shoulders until I could see them on either side of me.

This time, when Bird flapped his wings, it was a huge, powerful thing. He flapped once and my falling slowed.

Bird flapped his wings again and again, and then I wasn't falling at all.

Bird was still on me, *part* of me, but now he was holding me too. He beat his great black wings and we rose into the air.

I'd had falling dreams, but I'd had flying dreams too.

This feeling—this opposite of falling—was so much better than any dream.

Bird's wings were silent in the nothingness. Instead of flying us to the door, Bird landed me gently on the bridge, on the very spot I'd fallen from.

Pope was gone.

I didn't understand. "Bird," I whispered in case Pope could still hear my voice echo over the abyss, "take me all the way!"

But he was Bird-sized again and back on my shoulder. He beat his wings once. *No.*

"Please."

He ruffled his feathers and climbed up to the place where my neck met my shoulder and nuzzled me there. *No, it has to be you. You have to cross the bridge on your own. This is your journey, not mine.*

Bird hadn't let me fall, but it was my choice to keep going or not.

"I can't." I was crying, slow and quiet tears that hung from my chin.

A firm, tough-love kind of peck stopped my crying. *You can. Because you have to. Because you are brave.*

And I guess I was, because I pushed my shoulders back, ignored that insistent knot between them, and began to cross the bridge again.

I took a deep, shaking breath and let it out slowly.

The next breath shook just a little less.

By the third breath I was rising to my feet.

By the fourth, I was walking.

This time I was even slower, more careful than before. I went one step at a time, counting in my head.

One, two.

One, two.

One, two.

All the while, I fought off thoughts about Pope and Des and The Clackity and falling into the endless abyss. I pushed out everything except the bridge ahead of me and my feet beneath me and I focused and I counted.

One, two.

One, two.

One, two.

When I reached the other side, I collapsed on the stone floor of the sixth house. I think it was the adrenaline and fear and exhaustion all mixed together, but I trembled so hard I was basically a tiny earthquake.

I found the second bottle of water in my backpack and drank almost all of it. My hands were shaking so hard that the first sips mostly spilled down my chin. Bird was spinning and dancing across my back. He was almost as proud of me as I was.

"Buddy, it turns out little birds can be powerful all by themselves, too. I don't know . . . I just . . . thank you." There had to be better words than that, but those were the only ones I could find right then. I patted Bird gently, hoping he understood.

The nuzzle against my collarbone told me he did.

I wiped my mouth with the back of my arm and

started to laugh. It didn't last long. The sound of my laughter echoing around the sixth house and through the black nothing was scary instead of happy.

Something in me—something big and heavy—had shifted. I needed to think about it, needed to figure out what it was, because it felt important. But first I was getting out of the sixth house.

Pope hadn't bothered closing the back door. A piece of purple sky peeked through the gap between it and the frame. I pulled the heavy door open and took a deep breath. The gasoline-and-rosewater smell was back, and before me was another field of green-black grass.

And somewhere beyond it, the seventh house.

And somewhere in the seventh house, Aunt Des.

And probably Pope, too.

21

I'd never been *so* happy to see the sun, even
if it was a black sun in a violet sky.

The veranda on the front of the sixth house wrapped
all the way around to the back. Another set of steps led
down and into the sprawling field ahead. I stumbled
down those stairs on wobbly legs as fast as I could and
kept running until I was out of the shadow of the sixth
house.

The sun was warm, and when I turned to get a last
look, the sixth house was gone. I was glad.

There was no sixth house, no cobblestone alleyway or
impossibly tall and windowless walls.

I was surrounded by farmland. Wheat and corn and
other things I couldn't name reached up toward the only
sun they'd ever known and were the same color as the
grass. A silhouette of a barn stood in the distance, past
where the sixth house had been a minute before. I wasn't
about to be fooled by another paper cutout of a building.
I remembered the silhouette neighborhood before the
third house, and the way I'd almost lost myself there. I
wasn't desperate enough to risk that again.

In the opposite direction, the field rose in a gentle slope of a hill. I climbed it easily, and it was so good to be on the ground with the tall grasses brushing against my legs that I nearly started crying all over again. And I might have, except I reached into my pocket to jangle my collection of keys and it hit me like a hard punch—I didn't have a key to the seventh house.

I stopped, frozen.

I'd made a mistake.

I tried to think back to the last house, to the black horror of a room. There had been no sign of a key. The room held nothing but a bridge and an abyss and awful, pitiful, trapped things in the iron walls. The more I thought about it, the surer I was. If there was a key to the seventh house, I hadn't come across it yet. So I did the only thing I could do.

I kept walking.

At the top of the hill, the field flattened out and became a deep yard. In that yard was the seventh house.

From where I stood, it looked like any other farmhouse. Two stories tall and off-white, it was half-hidden behind a grove of trees that could have been giant old maples. A porch stretched across its front, and the door was painted a deep red.

The house was welcoming. It made me think of Dorothy coming home from Oz, of warm places filled with hardworking, happy families and laughter and busy kitchens.

But I also remembered the house the first time I'd seen it, with siding made of bones and curtains decorated with screaming skeletons instead of children or flowers. The seventh house was only pretending to be a home. It was something much worse, and I was about to go in and find out just what that was. Because Desdemona was in there somewhere, and I had to get to her before Pope did.

It crossed my mind that he already had, that I was too late. But I wasn't going to stop.

That was when I knew what the shifting feeling inside me had been, and why it mattered. It turned out that something changes inside you when your worst nightmare actually happens and you make it through. When you face your greatest fear and it doesn't kill you.

Losing Des was the thing that scared me most, but falling was the scariest thing that could happen to *me*. And it had happened. And I hadn't just fallen, I'd fallen into an endless abyss.

I'd fallen and I hadn't died. Because someone had helped me. Because Bird had saved me. And because then I'd made the decision and crossed the bridge on my own.

Des was still missing, but that wasn't happening to *me*. It was happening to Des. And now it was my turn to do the saving. That huge, scared thing inside me hadn't just shifted. It had been replaced by something fierce and brave and determined.

I would save her if I could. If I couldn't, I would make things as bad for Pope as possible. And then I'd find The Clackity and make things bad for it, too. I knew my thoughts were braver and fiercer than I was, but I let them take over anyway. Brave and fierce were what I needed, and they were a lot better than panicked and defeated.

Brave and fierce, but I also needed to be smart. I had an advantage and I needed to keep it. Pope, who had shoved me off the bridge, thought I was dead. I needed to make sure I didn't give him any reason to think otherwise.

My backpack was heavy with all the things I'd brought with me, and with the few items I'd collected since the day started. One of those was the rose-gold bell Pink had given me. She'd said, *Wear it when you want to be very quiet.*

I found the bell on its delicate chain. It jingled like music when it moved. There was nothing quiet about it, and I thought perhaps Pink hadn't enchanted it as well as she thought she had. I slipped it over my head and around my neck anyway.

When I did, something very interesting happened. The first thing I noticed was that the bell stopped jingling as soon as I put it on. I jumped up and down a little just to be sure. When I jumped, I couldn't hear myself in the long grass. For that matter, I couldn't hear my own breathing. Or my heartbeat in my ears.

I found a small stone in the dirt and tossed it. It thudded softly when it landed. So I could still hear, and other things still made sounds, but I didn't.

As an experiment, I tried to talk. Nothing came out, even though I could feel my vocal cords working. "Bird?" I asked with my silent words. "Can you hear me?"

He beat his wings once. *Yes.*

That was good. I wanted to be able to talk to my buddy, just in case. I didn't know if he would save me again, or if he even could. But he had more than once. Besides, he was good company.

I had the noise problem sorted out, but there was still the issue of being seen. That one was more complicated. I needed to get past Pope, but how was I supposed to become invisible? I ran through the things I knew about him, but they were all pretty awful and not helpful at all.

Focus.

Focus.

Focus.

Then I remembered what The Clackity had told me in the second house.

We'd been talking about the penny-eyed ghosts and it'd said, *The coins make it so he can't see them anymore.*

If the pennies kept Pope from seeing the ghosts, maybe they'd work for me, too. And it just so happened that I had two pennies in my pocket, thanks to my pretty guide. Two bright and shining wheat pennies, brand-new and a hundred years old all at the same time. I looked them over, but there was nothing special about them as far as I could tell.

Sitting in the tall grass, I closed my eyes and tried putting the pennies on my eyelids. They slipped right off. I tried a few more times, squinting and furrowing my brow as I did my best to make them stay. It didn't do any good, because even if they stayed put, my eyes would be shut. Pope might not be able to see me, but I wouldn't be able to see anything at all.

An idea came to me then, and it was pretty scary, but

it also seemed right. Maybe the pennies weren't meant to go *on* my eyes, but *in* them.

I didn't like the idea of putting pennies in my eyes—I didn't even like to touch my eyes to get something out of them when they itched. The whole idea gave me the full-body creeps.

I tried it anyway.

Part of my brain screamed that this was a terrible idea, but I pushed that voice back. My body was on board because my hands were steady and sure. At first I blinked too much and my eyes watered, and I couldn't make myself do it. It took a few tries before I was able to make my hand place the metal right against my eye. When I did, the first penny slipped onto my eye like I imagined a contact lens would. It was cold and tingled a little, but it fit like it was made just for me and didn't hurt at all.

I closed my penniless eye and realized I could still see through my penny eye. If anything, my vision was sharper than it had been before. The second penny was easier. After a couple of tries I got it into my left eye and blinked a few times.

I hadn't been imagining it. My vision, fine to begin with, was better. The colors around me were sharper, *more.* When I squinted up at the sun, I saw it wasn't truly black. Threads of every color swirled and swam on its surface. And around the sun was a rainbow like a halo.

I almost got Aunt D's mirrored compact out of her purse to get a good look at myself but changed my mind. I didn't really want to see myself with coins on—*in*—my eyes. It would be too much like a premonition of my own death, and that felt like a bad idea. I had to stay fierce and brave, not superstitious and scared.

I had a bell around my neck and pennies in my eyes and Bird on my shoulder.

I was as ready as I would ever be to go save my aunt.

22

I expected the seventh house to be made of bones, same as it had been when I first got to the neighborhood behind the abattoir. But as I got close, I could see it was now just white painted siding. The paint was chipped and peeling in places, and age-grey wood poked through. That didn't make me feel any better.

The house looked like a regular house, but that was just a disguise. The air around it didn't move, and even though we were in the middle of what looked like a farm, no birds sang, and no crickets chirped their cricket songs. It didn't cast any shadows at all, even though the black sun was at an angle behind it.

The house was a dead house.

It was worse than the sixth house in its own way, because at least the sixth house didn't pretend to be something it wasn't. Above the red door, in carefully painted letters, was a single word.

It looked like this:

POPE

So this was *his* house. And that meant while I had an advantage, he had one too.

The front door of John Jeffrey Pope's house was unlocked. The tarnished knob turned easily in my hand.

That was good, because it meant I didn't need to go hunting for the last key.

That was bad, because he was already here.

Even though I didn't have to worry about making noise thanks to the rose-gold bell, I stepped through the door as quietly as I could. I pulled it closed behind me and it clicked softly when it shut.

I stood for a minute, hoping for some sign of Desdemona. Her voice, or her perfume, or something.

Nothing.

Nothing but a feeling, deep in my stomach, that told me she was there somewhere. That I was close. It wasn't much to go on, but it was enough.

The room was just a living room. It had a couch and two chairs, all of them draped with handmade country quilts. The rug in the center of the room was oval and blue, and the wooden tables were dark wood and matched the china cabinet in the corner. There was nothing fancy about it, but it was clean, and it looked like the people who lived there loved it.

Aside from the china cabinet, it wasn't a very interesting room. But the cabinet was curious: it didn't hold plates or bowls or glasses. It was, in fact, nearly empty. Two of its three shelves were bare, not even dusty.

On the center shelf was an open, shiny black box, its lid attached by brass hinges. Inside the box were maybe a dozen tiny ceramic and fabric figures lined up like chess pieces. The biggest of them was almost three inches tall. The figures were all facedown on a black fabric cushion. Next to the box was a small cut-glass bowl. The bottom of the bowl was covered in grains of uncooked rice.

I didn't know what to make of any of it, so I left the cabinet behind and went to investigate the rest of the house. From the living room, there were two doors to choose from, one on the left wall and one on the right.

The door to the right was open, and through it was a big kitchen, as plain and clean as the living room. On the far side of the kitchen were a simple wooden table and chairs with room enough to seat eight people. All the chairs but one had been turned upside down on the table, their legs sticking up in the air like dead bugs. Only the chair at the head of the table was upright, and the place in front of it was set for a meal. Plates and silverware and a plaid cloth napkin were laid out, ready for someone to serve up breakfast. Or lunch or dinner. I had no idea what time it was, what meal was to be served next. It felt very, very late, but the sun still hadn't moved, and time didn't mean anything, except it meant *everything* because I knew I was running out of it.

Off the kitchen was an open door, and behind that a flight of stairs. The stairs led down into what had to be a basement, or, more likely in the old farmhouse, a cellar. I had no interest in going down those stairs. There was something—someone—down there. I could feel it, the way you can feel eyes following you even when you can't see who they belong to.

I stepped back from the door and right into one of the overturned chairs. It tilted dangerously and I stumbled as I caught it just before it slammed down on the hardwood kitchen floor. My knees hit the floor silently, but they still hit the floor and there was a change in the air, a vibration that came with the impact. I held tight to the leg of that chair, afraid to let go in case it toppled over.

Even Bird, who'd been fluttering all over my back in a nervous tizzy, froze.

Then there was a thump.

And another.

Someone was coming up the cellar stairs.

I counted the footsteps as they came, seven, eight, nine.

At ten footsteps, John Jeffrey Pope stood in the doorway. He turned his sandy head slowly, scanning the kitchen. I crouched, half-hidden under the table. The hand that held the chair leg was sweating so much I thought it would slip and the chair would come crashing down and I would be caught.

I didn't move or breathe. I willed the panic away, knowing that if I started shaking, the chair I held would start shaking too. My eyes watered under their penny lenses.

Pope stood still for a few seconds longer, looking and listening.

Then he turned and went back down the stairs.

I let my breath out, long and slow.

I counted his footsteps, and when I got to eight, nine,

ten, I let go of the chair and stood up. On tiptoes, I crept from the kitchen back into the living room, then to the closed door. It opened to another flight of stairs, which went up to the second floor. Old stairs always creaked, and I knew from my own house that the quietest parts were closest to the edges, so I clung to the wall as I climbed the stairs to look for Aunt Des.

A narrow hallway with four doors, two on either side, was at the top. All the doors were open, so I ducked into the first room. It held two twin-size beds covered in more handmade quilts, and a dresser with a big mirror. Next to each bed was a pair of brown men's work boots. The dresser mirror was draped in a black cloth, so I couldn't see myself even if I wanted to. Which I didn't.

The only decoration in the room was a framed photo that hung on the wall between the two beds. It was a photo I recognized because I'd seen it a thousand times before: five handsome brothers, square-jawed and narrow-eyed. At least the brothers who I could see. Pope was still there, second from the left, smiling his awful smile. The faces of the two brothers on either end had been cut out and replaced with pennies.

In Pope's world, dead people got pennies.

The fabric on the mirror made sense. I'd lived in Blight Harbor long enough to know that people sometimes covered mirrors with black cloths so that the spirits of the dead wouldn't get trapped in the glass. It was silly, a superstition.

Unless you lived in a town like Blight Harbor.

Or in a house like this.

In this house, it felt like the right thing to do. Someone smart had made sure the dead brothers didn't get trapped in the mirror while their ghosts wandered around, looking for wherever it was they would go next.

I yanked the black cloth off the mirror. I figured Pope's brothers were long gone, but maybe Pope would find his way to the mirror and get stuck there. When I pulled down the cloth, it kicked up a sharp, cold breeze. It lasted only a few seconds and was gone before I could give it much thought.

I turned away fast, not wanting to see myself with pennies in my eyes. Not quite fast enough, though, and I caught a glimpse of copper coins the same color as my hair where my eyes were supposed to be. It gave me goose bumps, and a shiver climbed all the way up my back and down my arms.

I didn't want to be in that room any longer. There was nothing there for me, anyway.

Down the hall, the second room was almost a replica of the first: two beds, two pairs of boots, and a black cloth over the mirror on the dresser. The same photo hung on the wall, but in this one all the brothers' faces had been replaced with pennies.

All but Pope's, that is.

I didn't know if Pope had killed his brothers, but that seemed likely.

One by one, I touched the pennies where the brothers' faces should have been. "I'm sorry for whatever happened to you. I can't fix it, but I have to try to help someone else. I hope you're okay, wherever you are."

I took the cloth off that mirror too. Another cold breeze stirred, and this time I knew I had done *something* by taking those cloths down. But what I had done, and whether it had been a mistake, I didn't know.

There were two bedrooms remaining, and I went into both. From that side of the hallway, the rooms faced the outside of the house and had windows that let in black sunlight filtered by ivory curtains.

The third bedroom had a single larger bed, its white bedspread pulled tight and neat around its corners. On the bed was a bouquet of roses and what might have been calla lilies. Once white, the flowers were yellow and brittle with age.

Calla lilies are funeral flowers. I learned that when I was eight, at the service for my parents who weren't dead. Just . . . missing.

A dark wooden cross hung over the bed and a small pair of lady's shoes rested on the floor. The dresser in what I guessed to be Mother Pope's room was larger than the others, and the mirror was covered in a black lace shawl. On the dresser was a picture of a young woman, pretty in a stern and strong sort of way. Maybe Mother Pope before she was Mother Pope, when she was just whoever she was before she had four boys and a monster.

The room made me sad. It made me think of moms gone and aunts missing. I left the shawl on the mirror. I didn't want to disturb the room any more than I already had.

The fourth and last bedroom had a single twin bed. The blanket and top sheet were turned down. No photo of smiling brothers, or of anyone else, hung on the wall. There was no cloth over the dresser mirror because the mirror wasn't there. It had been removed, and only the oval frame remained. There was a mason jar half-full of bright, shining pennies on the dresser.

There were no boots on the floor because Pope had them on.

I went over every inch of the room as fast as I could. There was no sign of Des anywhere. She wasn't in any of the bedrooms. She hadn't been in the living room, or in the kitchen. I still had that deep-in-my-stomach feeling that Des was somewhere close, that I was almost there—almost had her back.

There was only one place left to look. It turned out I was going down the cellar stairs after all.

"You ready, buddy?" I asked Bird with my silent words.

He flapped *Yes*. But he shuddered a little too.

23

Sneaking downstairs is harder than sneaking up them. I don't know why, but it's true.

I went down the fourteen stairs back to the first floor of Pope's house, willing my feet to be soft and my body light. I might not have made any noise thanks to my magic bell, but those were creaky old steps.

Back in the living room, I pulled the door to the staircase nearly shut behind me. I didn't want to give any hint that I was in the house, and wished I had thought about it before I went up to investigate the second floor. But, I reasoned, if I had closed the door behind me on the way up, I would have had to open it again when I came back down.

I shivered as I imagined opening that door only to find Pope there waiting patiently, hands in his pockets and smiling.

I went back through the kitchen and to the top of the cellar stairs. I stood and listened. Whistling, soft and tuneless, carried up the cellar steps.

Pope was still down there.

I didn't know anything about the cellar. Was it big

like a regular basement, or as small as a crawl space? Would there be a way for me to sneak down undetected, or would I have no choice but to squeeze right past Pope? Was it dark down there, or was there some source of light? Did ghosts even need light to see? I didn't think they did, but I put it on my list of things to ask Des.

Everything in me said going down into that cellar with Pope was a mistake. I was running out of time—I could feel it in my bones. I could feel it in that awful house. But even though the clock was ticking, I'd have to wait for him to come upstairs.

Unless.

Unless I could make him leave the cellar. But bringing attention to myself was the last thing I wanted to do, so I had to draw his attention somewhere else.

The plates on the kitchen table were white and shiny, and best of all, they were heavy.

I grabbed the smaller in one hand and the dinner plate in the other. I crept to the door between the kitchen and the living room. I threw the smaller plate first and it landed with a thud on the oval-shaped blue rug. It was loud, but maybe not loud enough to carry to the cellar.

I held the dinner plate like a Frisbee in my right hand and winged it at the front door. It went wild and sailed to the left, crashing into the china cabinet. The glass door on the right exploded.

That was certainly loud enough.

I jogged on the balls of my feet to the old stove and crouched next to it, getting as small as I could get.

Pope came storming up the stairs, eyes wild. No

whistling now. He ran into the living room and I ran across the kitchen and to the cellar door. The steps were concrete and didn't protest when I thudded down them. As I went, it occurred to me there were too many steps. I remembered hearing Pope walk up maybe ten of them. Now there were easily thirty.

At the bottom of the stairs was the poured concrete floor of a cellar, but the room was much bigger than it had any right to be. The ceiling was high, vaulted even. And I couldn't see where the room ended. The walls of the cellar were somewhere past the limits of the house, but they were hidden in shadows so thick and black that the rest of the room was lost beyond them.

The only source of light was an oil lamp on a workbench, which stood ten feet away from the last stair. It was like an island in the black expanse. If Des was down there, I'd need the lamp to investigate the rest of the room.

I rushed to the workbench, trying not to think about what might be watching from those shadows. As I put my fingers around the metal ring of the lamp, two things occurred to me: First, I couldn't take the lamp with me. Its light would give away my location in the dark. Second, this was no regular workbench.

The surface had a white cloth draped over it, probably a bedsheet. And on top of that were tools, but they were very small. Too small for regular work. The tools—clippers and pliers and delicate sewing shears—belonged on a jeweler's table, not in a slaughterhouse worker's impossible cellar. In the very center of the bench, something was covered in a clean white handkerchief.

I picked up the corner of the cloth, then dropped it. I didn't want to look under the handkerchief. I was certain I would find a small animal or something even worse. Whatever was under there was something I wouldn't be able to unsee.

I could still hear Pope stomping around the main floor, slamming doors, and then heavy feet going up the stairs to the second floor with the bedrooms. I had a little time, but probably not much.

Bird nipped my shoulder. *Do it now. He'll be back soon.*

I took a deep, quaking breath and gingerly lifted the handkerchief. I almost laughed when I saw what was underneath.

It was a doll.

I almost cried when I saw who it was.

It was my aunt Desdemona.

The Desdemona doll had long black hair and silver jewelry painted onto her fair skin, and she wore the same black summer dress I'd last seen her in when she disappeared into the stun shaft.

There was also a small black case on the table, the kind you put rings in, and inside the case were two shining copper coins. They were a tenth the size of regular pennies, but that's what they were. Pennies.

I knew then what the dolls in the china cabinet were. *Who* they were. And I thought I knew what was really in the cut-glass bowl, and it wasn't rice. My heart shriveled into a rotten black peach pit. If Des was here, and was a doll, I was too late. I scooped her up gently, trying not to snap any of her fragile limbs.

But she was warm. As warm as me. And when I put the porcelain Des doll up to my ear, the tiniest of heartbeats—a hummingbird's heart—thrummed in her chest. If the rose-gold bell wasn't silencing my own heart, I never would have heard hers.

Still alive. Somehow.

Maybe I was in time after all.

Tears that were happy and sad and a dozen other things dripped down my face. "Hi, Des. I'm gonna get you out of here. Sorry it took so long." I wrapped my aunt in the handkerchief and put her in my backpack, wrapping her again in my black sweatshirt to pad her as best I could. I closed the ring case with the dollhouse pennies and dropped it into my bag as well. I hoped it would be enough, that she would be safe enough, because I didn't have time to do more.

Heavy footsteps crossed the living room, then the kitchen, and then, too soon, started down the cellar stairs. I swallowed my fear and slipped into the shadows. I knew Pope couldn't see me, but hiding was an instinct. I couldn't just stand there in the light of the oil lamp, exposed.

Pope stopped at the bottom of the stairs, as alert as a guard dog. Then he began to sniff the air. I wasn't wearing perfume or fancy lotion, but I hadn't had a shower in at least two days. And the way I was sweating, there was no way he wouldn't be able to smell me.

Pope stopped at his workbench and placed his hands

on the empty space where the Desdemona doll had been. Without warning, he began to pound his fists against the table, hard enough to break them or it. The sound echoed through the endless cellar. He stopped just as suddenly as he had started and ran his hands through his hair, composing himself. Somehow, the calm was scarier than the rage.

He got very still and picked up the sewing shears.

Then he began to move toward me. I took a step backward with every step he took closer. Eventually, I would run into a wall and would be trapped. Then I would have to hope I was fast enough to get around him and up the stairs and out the front door and out of the neighborhood and across the field and to the abattoir and . . .

And the panic was back.

I didn't know how to fight it and avoid him all at the same time. It rose up like a wave, filling me and making it hard to do anything but shake. Soon I wouldn't be able to take any more steps without my knees giving out, and then I really would be trapped.

I expected every step backward to be my last one, and then I took a step and bumped into something. But it wasn't a wall. It was a person. Bigger and taller than me. I felt a hand reach around my face, and a cold, rough finger press itself to my lips.

That finger told me, *Shhh.*

I didn't *shhh.* I screamed a silent scream while the hand pushed me back, deeper into the shadows. Bird tried to calm me with gentle wing strokes on my back. Maybe it helped, but I think I was really just scared out of my panic. I didn't blink under my pennies and couldn't have closed my eyes if I wanted to, because my whole body had gone rigid with fear. That meant I didn't miss a bit of what happened next.

The man I'd run into emerged from the shadows, along with three other figures, all of them wider and taller than Pope. All of them had handsome, sun-worn faces. All of them had pennies in their eyes. They were Pope's brothers. The ghosts of his brothers.

I knew Pope couldn't see them, but I think he *felt* them, because I did too. They were like a cold and swirling wind, heavy with full storm clouds and lightning waiting to strike. So I hadn't imagined the chilly breezes back in the brothers' bedrooms. They had been trapped in the mirrors after all. When I'd pulled down the black cloths, I'd released them.

Pope's face changed. He smiled, but it wasn't a real smile. It was a *Please, boys, why don't we sit down and talk about this?* afraid kind of smile. The brothers approached him, and he retreated, back to the door, then up the stairs.

I moved then, not wanting to lose sight of Pope.

I followed them up the stairs, keeping a few steps between me and the family reunion. Once he was in the kitchen, Pope started toward the living room, still backing away from the presence of his four bigger brothers.

I slipped past them and made my way silently to the front door.

One of the brothers, the one I'd run into, looked at me with his penny eyes and gestured for me to get going.

"Thank you."

The man couldn't hear me, but he understood. He nodded once, then returned his attention to his youngest brother.

I glanced at the shattered china cabinet door, and at the box and bowl inside. Now that I knew who the dolls were, it was impossible not to recognize them. They were my penny-eyed ghosts from the third house. And I was willing to bet the rice in the bowl would prove to be a collection of porcelain fingers and toes.

Without overthinking it, I grabbed the box out of the broken cabinet. I poured the porcelain fragments from the bowl into the box and closed the lid. I clutched it to my chest as I made for the door.

I spared one look at Pope. His eyes were locked onto me. He might not have been able to see *me*, but he could see that box in my arms. For all intents and purposes, I was no longer invisible, but I couldn't take it back now even if I wanted to.

Pope's eyes burned and he no longer looked frightened. He was angry and, I thought, hungry.

I threw the door open, heaved myself out of it, and didn't look back.

PART THREE

⌒∼◦∼⌒

Count All the Fingers,
Count All the Toes

24

Off the porch, down the front steps, and onto
a green-black lawn, I ran from Pope's house as fast as I
could.

I was back in the neighborhood. All seven houses sat
in their neat semicircle. They looked almost . . . regular.
But I knew better. The houses were kind of like people in
that way—their outsides didn't always match the secrets
they kept inside.

Ahead, the tall iron gate split the field beyond.

But something had changed. The black sun, steady
in the sky all day, was sinking toward the horizon. The
purple sky was darkening into swirling shades of indigo
and navy, creating a kaleidoscope of color that would
have been beautiful if it had not been a warning written
in the sky: time was running out, *and fast*.

Time, which hadn't passed all day, was now a flipped
hourglass with only a few grains of sand left to fall.

*Safe in houses. Safe until the field. And best before
the sun goes down.* The Clackity's words ran through my
head, over and over again. It had lied about being safe
in houses, and it might have lied about the sun. It didn't

matter. The idea of being in that neighborhood after dark was scary, no matter how many lies The Clackity told.

There was no telling how long the four brothers could keep Pope occupied. I had to get moving.

Between me and the gate was that awful haze, the misty film that had made me think terrible things when I first went through it. I very badly did not want to go through that haze again, but there wasn't any other way to the gate.

As I got closer, something caught my eye. The front door of the third house was open, and from it figures emerged. One after another, a dozen penny-eyed ghosts left the house. I glanced from Pope's house back to the approaching ghosts, terrified of one and curious about the others.

The ghosts moved quickly, shuffling and stumbling as they came. When they reached me, my pretty guide was in the lead. She was followed closely by the tall man in the hat that The Clackity had taken over until Bird drove him out.

My favorite penny-eyed ghost stopped in front of me. She put one hand on the doll box and the other on the side of my face. Then she went toward the haze.

I yelled out to warn her, but the rose-gold bell was still on. I yanked at it and broke the delicate chain. The whole thing went into my pocket, and then I did yell, "Stop! It's bad!"

But even as I shouted, the mist pulled back. It came close to my friend but didn't touch her. One by one, the other penny-eyed ghosts stopped long enough to touch the doll box, and to touch me. Then each made their way into the haze. As they did, they pushed the fog back a little more. Soon, the ghosts were standing in two rows of six, holding the mist back.

There was a clear path between me and the gate.

I didn't think twice.

I walked down the ghost path, clutching the box full of dolls. As I moved past the gate and into the field, the penny-eyed souls came with me. Each nodded my way as they left the neighborhood behind. Somehow, by taking the doll box with me, I was freeing them from that place.

Another thing happened as I left the gate.

The pennies fell from my eyes and landed on the ground at my feet. I'd gotten used to them and blinked as my vision righted itself. I stopped at the edge of the field long enough to put the pennies into my pocket, and the box of ghost dolls into my backpack. I had to rearrange things to make it fit, which took seconds to do, but it might as well have been hours.

The sun was setting faster than I liked.

As I put the box in my bag, the penny-eyed ghosts each went their own way across the field. Only my pretty guide and the tall man left together. She looked over her shoulder and waved to me, then made an exaggerated movement with her hand. *Get going. You're not safe yet.*

That brought me back to focus. The ghosts had left, disappeared into the growing night, but I was not alone. Little black silhouettes danced around me.

Bird beat his wings joyfully at being reunited with his friends. The flock of shadow sparrows from the abattoir had waited for me. For *us*. I was absurdly happy to see them.

"Little buddies! Let's go home!"

But Bird's joyful flapping changed, became erratic, even as I spoke. And the flock of shadow birds stopped dancing. Bird pecked me as hard as he ever had, enough to draw blood. *He's coming. Go.*

The haze had closed back up after the penny-eyed ghosts passed through it. Behind the thick air stood a familiar form.

I'd wasted too much time and could only pray the haze had an effect on him, that it wouldn't part for Pope the way it had for his victims. It had been bad for me, and I was mostly a pretty good person. I hoped it was horrible for him.

I was running even as I thought all those things. Running toward the abattoir, which loomed in the distance, black against the darkening sky. As I ran, something gnawed at my mind. I was making a mistake, but I wasn't sure what mistake it was. Then the grumpy witch sister Grey's words came flooding back to me. She'd warned me about The Clackity, and about Pope. She'd said, *They're both dangerous alone, but you don't want to bring them together.*

And I was leading Pope straight to The Clackity.

I kept running, but I slowed a little. I risked a glance back and saw that Pope had made it through the haze, though he was on his knees, just as I'd been my first time through. I didn't know if ghosts could vomit, but it looked like that one was.

Good. I hope you choke, I thought.

My run became a jog as a plan came together. It wasn't a very good plan, but it was the only one I had. It depended on a lot of things I couldn't be sure of, and it depended on timing.

I stopped in the green-black field, almost all black now that the light was nearly gone. I dropped my backpack and pulled out Aunt D's purse. Thankfully, it had ended up on top, right under the sweatshirt holding the Desdemona doll, when I rearranged things to make room for the box. I rummaged through the purse until I found a small vial. The salt in it glowed bright white.

Bird was frantic. *Go!*

"I know what I'm doing," I lied.

The other shadow birds buzzed around me like confused bees.

I opened the vial. The cork made a popping sound as it came out. I began to pour the salt into what I hoped was a close approximation of a circle, a circle maybe six feet across. It needed to be big enough for me and one other person. Big enough that there'd be a bit of room between us.

The vial shouldn't have held enough salt to make the circle, but it did. Because of something Des, or even Lily, had done to it. Because they'd magicked it just like I knew—*hoped*—they had.

In case you don't know about salt circles, let me tell you: they're old, powerful magic. The kind of magic anyone can do. According to Aunt Des and Lily, nothing supernatural can get past a barrier made of salt. If you make a complete circle out of it, nothing bad can get in. If you trap a bad thing in a salt circle, it can't get out.

It's simple.

And easy to mess up.

If the circle is broken anywhere, it won't work, and you might as well just hold up your hands and surrender to whatever it is that's trying to get you. But that danger didn't matter, because this was the best idea I had. The only idea, really.

I stood in the center of the circle, while Bird had a conniption back and forth across my shoulders. His shadow friends were in a frenzy. They took turns dive-bombing me, trying to force me to move, to *Go! Run! Now!* I gently swatted at them to keep them out of my face and my hair.

I didn't run.

I stood my ground, surrounded by apoplectic shadow birds and a thin ring of salt. Pope was approaching, no sauntering or whistling now. He wasn't running, but he was *fast*. He flickered in and out of view like he was moving under a strobe light.

I blinked, and he had cut the distance between us in half.

I blinked, and he was close enough that I could see the straight line of his mouth and the angry greed in his eyes.

I blinked, and he was just outside the salt circle, the sewing shears still in his hand.

Pope looked at the line of salt just beyond his toes. It was just salt, nothing magical about it. It wouldn't hold him. I saw it, and I knew he saw it too.

When his eyes met mine, they were crinkly around the edges. His smile was big and there was nothing handsome left in it.

Pope lifted one boot-covered foot and stepped into my failed ring of protection.

As he stepped in, I stepped backward, out of my useless barrier.

We were so close to each other that I could smell him. That cave-and-grave smell I'd first noticed when I'd left the abattoir for the green-black field hung around him like bad cologne. He reached out to me with one hand and I ducked away.

Then Pope lunged at me with his wicked, sharp little scissors. They whooshed over my head as I stepped out of the circle.

He might have had me, but the flock of shadow sparrows went on the attack. They dove and pecked, and where they scratched him, no blood ran. Instead little rips opened up in his clothes and his skin. And in those tears, I could see the black nothing of the abyss. Pope flailed and struck out, but the birds weren't deterred. They skirted his clumsy blows only to return and attack again.

In my right hand, I cupped the tiny vial of salt. As I dodged Pope's wild swings, I poured a little more out and closed the gap I'd intentionally left in the circle.

The effect was immediate and blinding.

The salt circle, now complete, glowed like sunlit snow. From it grew crystal tendrils, thorny vines crawling straight up into the air. They wrapped through and around each other, twisting into a kind of birdcage, where they met at the top.

And inside the cage stood Pope.

Until that moment, Pope had never spoken a word to me. He'd never made a sound aside from his whistling. But now he wailed. It was wild and guttural and carried across the fields and up into the air. I knew the sound was real because in the distance, dogs began to bark and howl in response.

Pope threw the sewing shears straight at me in a last desperate attempt to end my life. They sailed through a gap in the bars of the glowing cage and stuck into the ground like a dart, coming to rest at the toes of my shoes. I snatched them out of the grass and tossed them into the pouch on the side of my backpack meant to hold water bottles. I didn't really want them, but I *really* didn't want Pope to have them either.

I had no idea how long the salt circle would hold him, and I didn't stick around to find out. As the last light of the black sun slipped below the horizon, it exploded in a violent rainbow of colors—the same colors I'd seen in the sun when I had pennies in my eyes.

I snatched up my backpack and ran then, black high-tops pounding the blackened field, through the dark night toward the even darker abattoir that waited for me.

25

I ran until I reached the sagging wood ramp, the one that led to the stun shaft. The same path that animals would have taken on their way to the slaughter-house.

Breathing hard, I stopped and tried to work through what I would have to do next. I didn't have a flashlight or a lantern or even a candle. Nothing to help me see in the coming black.

Except . . .

Except, maybe I did.

I set my backpack on the ground and opened it just enough to get my hand in, afraid of spilling any of its contents on the ground and losing them in the strange grass. I rummaged around, hoping I could find it by feel— hoping I wasn't jostling Des around too much. Pope's howls still carried across the field and made it hard to concentrate on anything but getting very far away.

When my fingers brushed something long and thin, I knew I'd found it. Carefully, slowly, so as not to break it, I pulled the oversized matchstick out of my bag. Gold had given it to me with the words, *You can use it only once, so use it well.* I hoped I was making the right decision, that I had chosen the right time. I also hoped I could find something to strike it on.

I felt around the ground until my fingers found a long, flat rock. I brushed it off in case any dirt or grass was stuck on it. Then I took a deep breath, said a little half prayer, and dragged the head of the match against it.

The match lit, which was a surprise.

Then it changed even as I held it in my hand, which was a bigger surprise.

The match grew, became heavier, and before I could blink, it was a two-foot wand with flames pouring out of the top. The light the flames threw was warm and gold, and the night pulled away from that light like a cowering thing.

I could see then that my sparrow friends had followed me across the field. They danced in the gold glow, and Bird turned happy circles on my back.

I had my little friends.

I had a light.

I had Pope in a cage.

I had a backpack full of liberated ghosts.

I had Des—I hoped.

I was as ready as I'd ever be to face The Clackity.

Walking up that long, creaking ramp was bad. Each step landed in the invisible hoofprints of ten thousand animals, all of them going to the last place they'd ever see. My skin crawled and I shoved the thought away. I was giving myself the creeps, and the situation was creepy enough as it was.

The path led directly into the steel stun shaft. My feet clanked against the metal floor and I wished my bell weren't broken. Inside, the gold flames made the tunnel almost cheerful.

Almost.

The sparrows no longer danced. They were serious and in formation.

The ladder still stood where I'd left it, propped against the edge of the shaft. I was glad I wouldn't be jumping to the ground below. From my height, ten feet above the floor of the abattoir, I had a clear view out the wide mouth of the door on the far side. It was night out there, too. Time had passed on both sides of the slaughterhouse, but how much time I wasn't sure.

I held the torch in one hand and used the other to climb slowly down. When I reached the bottom, I stood still and silent, listening. For the longest time, there was nothing. For a fierce few seconds I thought maybe The Clackity had gotten bored, or maybe even lost back on the island of the Mother Witch tree. Maybe its part of my story was over.

"Pretty Penny! We are glad to welcome her home." The voice came from all around. The bright ember of hope turned into a cold, heavy chunk of coal in the pit of my stomach.

I turned in circles, looking into dark corners, trying to spot The Clackity in all that black.

"We don't like the yellow witchy light. We wish she would put it out so we can have a sit and talk."

"I'll stand, thank you. I'm not staying."

"Oh, maybe yes and maybe no. Maybe she will stay and tell The Clackity about her adventures. Maybe she has brought us a prize. Or maybe we will eat her."

The Clackity's face emerged from the dark like smoke coalescing into solid form. It was too close to mine, leaning down so that we stood eye to eye. Even in the gold light of the torch, its skin was pallid and grey.

I backed away a couple of steps but didn't look over my shoulder to the door. When I made a break for it, I wanted it to be a surprise.

"I did what you told me to do. I got through all the houses. I got past Pope. And I made it back before the sun went down. Almost."

"Oh, but she doesn't have her auntie, does she? Where is the pretty raven-haired lady?" The Clackity's broken smile grew wider, like it had thought of something funny. "Did the Cow and Piggy Man get her first? Oh, so sad for our Pretty Penny. She was not such a lucky penny then, was she?"

The Clackity made to touch my face, or maybe my hair, and I pulled away. At the same time, Bird flew across my back and up my shoulders, and, wings wide, spread himself like a mask across my eyes.

Having my Bird mask on was like wearing reverse sunglasses. Everything in the abattoir was brighter, the shadows thinner. I could see The Clackity, all of it, for the first time. It had too many arms and too many legs, but most of them hung limply from its sides. When Clackity recoiled from Bird, it pulled six useless arms and six useless legs with it. Its body was a twist of torsos, and three extra heads lolled at its sides. The Clackity's extra parts weren't solid. They might have been made of papier-mâché, or wasps' nests. The Clackity was a broken, dying sort-of spider.

"Pretty Penny has a nasty stain! Get the birdie away from The Clackity. Make it leave. We don't like it. We can't *stand* it."

"Bird stays. He's my friend. And we're leaving."

"Not leaving, not yet now. Where is The Clackity's prize? Where is the Cow and Piggy Man?"

"Pope? I left him in the field. He's probably still there, stuck in a salt cage. You can go get him. I don't think he's getting out soon."

The Clackity began to gibber, hot rage filling its one good eye. "We made a good, fair deal! Pretty Penny *shook* on it. We promised you your auntie, you promised us our Cow and Piggy Man present."

"We never shook on it." I backed away slowly, trying to distract it with words as I put some distance between us. "You wouldn't shake because of Bird, remember? Plus, you don't know my name and you need a name for a bargain. *And* you lied! Why do you want Pope, anyway? He's worse than you are . . . I think."

"Because we are all alone!" The Clackity wailed. It lifted one of the wasp-nest arms with its good left hand. "All the others have moved on, and now they are only shells, so much skin for us to carry around. The Cow and Piggy Man is smart, and he is wicked. He would help us get rid of the empty parts and we wouldn't be lonely. We would be strong again, and wicked like him."

"I don't know what you're talking about, but he's out there if you want him. Go get him. You deserve each other."

"We cannot go in the field!" The Clackity screamed. "We are not allowed! The girl child will go get him now and bring him back. Or she will be our new prize instead, even if she is nasty and ruined."

The Clackity lunged, skittering on its two good feet and two good hands.

An army of bird silhouettes flew from the shadows straight at the charging thing. They attacked Clackity the way they'd attacked Pope. But Clackity was faster than Pope, and it smashed them out of the air as they scratched and tore. Inside The Clackity, in the places the birds managed to strike, was the same black emptiness that had filled Pope. The same swirling black that was behind the strange neighborhood I'd spent my day in.

The Clackity was an abyss, full of absolutely nothing at all.

I ran then. I ran for the door and heard the skittering feet behind me.

Close.

Closer.

Too close.

I was never going to make it.

With just a few yards between me and the door, I turned to face The Clackity. It had gone fully mad. There was nothing human left in its face. I could never outrun it, and I knew there was no reasoning with it now, if there ever had been a chance for that.

I did the last thing I could.

I threw the torch at it. It missed, landing on the floor just in front of the creature.

But the torch didn't sputter and go out.

It erupted.

Like they were eating spilled gasoline, the flames of the torch began to spread. They crawled across the floor and up one wall of the abattoir. Somehow, the old, mostly stone building was burning like dry wood.

The Clackity keened, a sound like a hundred things in mourning.

"Wicked, nasty girl," it whined above the cracking, burning noise. "We will see her again. We will get our prize and come find her together."

The Clackity scuttled to the nearest drain in the concrete floor. The drain was far too small for the creature, but it began to squeeze in anyway. As it went headfirst down the drain, crunching, squelching sounds came from its empty arms and legs. They cracked and bent at weird angles as The Clackity pulled them through the drain to wherever it was going next. Its shadow refused to go with it. A thousand black spiders scattered, disappearing into the seams of the abattoir, click-click-clicking as they fled.

It was awful, maybe the worst thing I'd seen all day, and I didn't watch the end of it. The flames were too hot, the light too bright, and I was done.

I ran out the abattoir door, one bird over my eyes, and a flock of shadow sparrows—a smaller flock than before—followed at my heels.

Outside the fiery slaughterhouse, I collapsed in the grass. It was brown and green and prickly, just like it was supposed to be. The moon, white and round, hung in a sky I understood.

Bird crawled back to my shoulder. His friends landed all around me, some of them perched on my legs and my arms.

We sat together and watched the abattoir burn.

26

We didn't sit for long.

I wasn't about to get caught in front of a burning building—at the scene of a fire I'd set. The flames lashed high and bright. I turned in a giant circle, looking into the distance. There would be sirens at any time.

There was a neighborhood—a real neighborhood—not far from the abattoir. Someone would call the fire department, sooner rather than later. There was no way anyone would believe my story, and I'd end up waiting even longer to go home because I'd be in jail.

In the star-speckled night, I saw my bike, still where I'd left it, in the dirt behind Aunt D's car. Her car would be a problem. I had no idea how we'd explain what it was doing there, but I trusted that Desdemona would figure something out.

If she could.

My relief at being out of the abattoir disappeared into the air. I was out safe, but I wasn't so sure Des was. She was, after all, a doll wrapped in a sweatshirt in my backpack. I didn't know what to do next, how to help her if she could be helped. But I knew who might.

I got up from the ground. My whole body hurt with sunburn and hunger and exhaustion. My knees begged me to sit back down, but I couldn't. It might have been the middle of the night, but the endless day wasn't over quite yet.

I pulled my bike off the ground and got on. I pedaled down the drive and was heading down the street, gaining speed and feeling a little looser, when I realized my helmet was still back there somewhere on the abattoir lawn. If anyone found a plain black helmet, the kind tons of kids wore, chances were they wouldn't know for sure it was mine. I figured it wouldn't make for very good evidence of my crime. I didn't even think about going back for it. Aunt Des would never know I'd ridden without it, and if she found out, I figured she'd forgive me. Besides, it was maybe the twenty-seventh-most dangerous thing I'd done that day.

The streets were quiet, no sirens and no one yelling at me to stop and explain what I had done, why I was out on the streets at that hour (whatever hour it was). Maybe it was even later than I thought, and everyone was fast asleep.

The trip across town took no time at all. My head was full of the day that had just happened, of the things that I had done, and of the one important thing I'd failed to do. My mind was so busy that I was surprised when I turned down the street that led to the familiar little brown house.

I left my bike in the driveway between the garage and the parked beige car. But before I went to the door, there was something I had to do.

I knelt on the driveway, opened my backpack, and found my black sweatshirt. I held my breath. I unrolled the sweatshirt and unwrapped the handkerchief. It was one of the scariest things I had ever done.

What if I'd broken her?

What if she was cold?

The Desdemona doll was as tiny and fragile as I remembered. She was so light in my hands. But she was whole, and warm. I felt like I'd been crying all day and might never stop. I kissed the top of her head. "We're almost there. We're going to fix you." I put my aunt back in the handkerchief, and then my sweatshirt, and wrapped her up but didn't return her to my backpack. I clutched the bundle against my chest.

At the front door, I hesitated. How was I going to explain any of this? How could I make someone else believe me? I lifted my free hand to knock, but before I could, the door swung open. Warm light spilled out along with the smell of incense and maybe cookies.

Lily Littleknit peered at me through her thick glasses. "Evie Von Rathe! What are you doing here this late? What did you do to your hair? Does Desdemona know where you are?" Lily stopped and in a softer voice asked, "Is Des okay? Are *you* okay?"

I started more than crying then. I sobbed so ugly and so hard I thought I'd never stop. I had so much to tell Lily, but my words were all choked up and broken.

Lily put an arm around my shoulders and moved me through the front door. She took a long look outside, up and down the dark street, before she closed the door behind her.

And locked it.

Lily got me to her overstuffed, chocolate-colored couch and sat quietly with me until I calmed down enough to talk.

"I don't know where to start," I told her. I knew I needed to give her Des. I needed Lily to see so she could fix my aunt, but I wasn't ready. Because if Lily couldn't do it, if she couldn't fix Desdemona, I wasn't ready to know that yet.

"At the beginning, of course. But not yet." Lily left for her small kitchen and came back with two steaming mugs and a plate with a half-dozen brownies piled on it. The tea was hot, and the brownies were still warm. Like she'd been expecting me. And she probably had, or had been expecting *someone*, anyway.

Witches are weird like that.

I'd never been so glad for a cup of tea. Even though, at first, it made me cry all over again because I knew Des would have made me tea too.

Lily was patient. She let me calm down before she asked me again to tell her. I started to explain as best I could. Mostly Lily just listened, but she stopped me every now and then when she didn't understand.

"Ghosts," she asked, "with missing fingers and pennies in their eyes?"

"Missing toes, too," I reminded her.

"There were three witches, sisters?"

"Yeah. And I turned their mom into a tree."

"How did you fly after you'd fallen off the bridge?"

"I didn't, not really. Bird did. He saved me." Bird was

curled up where my throat met my chest, fast asleep. When Lily touched him with soft fingers, he stirred but didn't wake up. Poor little buddy was exhausted.

When I got to the part about the Desdemona doll on the workbench, Lily grew very serious and quiet. "And you have her?"

"Yeah. She's . . . she's here."

The whole time we talked I'd been clutching my sweatshirt against my chest. Now I set it on my lap and unfolded everything carefully.

Des rested, so tiny and fragile, in the middle of all that fabric. My aunt, my best person, small and warm and somehow alive when I handed her to Lily with trembling hands.

"Oh, Desdemona," Lily said sadly.

"Can you . . . can you fix her?"

"Perhaps."

It was only one word, *perhaps*, but it was like a sledgehammer to my stomach.

Now there were tears in Lily's eyes too. "Did you bring anything with you from that place? The house you found her in or anywhere else?"

I nodded as I emptied my pockets and my bag. Tried to breathe. On the living room table, I set out a small, strange collection:

Six keys—steel, candy, brass, glass, wood,
   and gold.
One rose-gold bell on a broken chain.
Two pennies.

One flower from the Mother Witch tree.

It hadn't wilted at all.

Two dollhouse pennies.

That was everything. Nearly. I hoped it was enough.

I told Lily all of it. Well, almost all of it. I didn't tell her about my box of penny-eyed dolls. They felt like a secret I was supposed to keep. At least for the time being.

Lily ran her hands over the objects, picking them up and putting them back down, murmuring to herself the whole time. Finally she turned and spoke to me. "You, my dear, need to get some rest."

"I can't sleep! Can you fix her? You have to fix her!"

"I'm going to do my best. But it is going to be an ugly business, and you'll have no part of it."

"But *Lily!*"

"Hush. Enough. You've had a very long day. Maybe two days long if I'm doing the math right. You are going to bed. I have to call someone."

"Who?"

"I'll tell you later. Now, off with you."

She took my hand and helped me off the couch, and we went to her guest room. Lily sent me into the attached bathroom to wash up as best I could while she found me something to sleep in. When I was done and dressed in a very old-fashioned nightgown that dragged on the ground, I crawled into bed. I'd never be able to sleep.

Lily turned out the light on her way out but left the lamp burning on the nightstand. I didn't want to be alone in the dark. Before she closed the door, she said, "By the way, kiddo, I like your hair." It was her way of saying, *I'm proud of you, you did good, I love you.*

Despite my heavy eyes and heavier heart, I smiled. "Thanks. Love you too, Lily." The door was almost closed when I called out one more time. "Lily?"

She opened it up a bit. "What, honey?"

"Help her, okay? She's my whole family."

Lily nodded. When she spoke, her voice cracked a little. "I'll try, honey. I'll do my very best."

Then the door was closed.

Then I was alone, a sleeping Bird snoring softly on my neck.

27

I was tired all the way into the insides of my bones, but it didn't matter. There was no way I was going to sleep. My brain was too busy. What if I lost the last of my family because I wasn't brave or smart or fast enough to save her? I hadn't been able to find my parents, and maybe I'd lost Desdemona, and everyone I loved kept slipping through my fingers like fog.

Maybe Lily would let me live with her. I could earn my keep at the library. Maybe I'll lose her, too, and be all by myself.

This was prime panic time, but I had used it all up. Maybe not for good, but at least for the time being. For one very long and weird and scary day, I'd been on a quest with a single goal—saving Aunt Desdemona. Now that I almost had, I was supposed to take a nap?

Nope.

I got out of bed and went into the living room. In the kitchen, Lily was busy doing something noisy. Whether it was making more tea or trying to fix Des, I had no idea.

I was creeping through the quiet room toward the

kitchen when someone knocked on the front door. Three times.

Pope.

I opened my mouth to scream for Lily, but she was already crossing the living room to the front door. I managed a squeaky, "Don't open it!"

Lily scrunched up her forehead, simultaneously put out and confused. "You're supposed to be in bed. And I told you I was calling someone." She threw open the door and I rushed to her side. To protect her or me, I wasn't sure.

Across the threshold, in the yellow porch light, were Grey, Pink, and Gold.

"Come in, cousins." Lily moved out of the way to let them through the door.

I stood there like a useless statue. The witch sisters were the last people I'd expected to see on Lily's front porch. But they were also the *best* people I could have hoped to see. If anyone could help Lily, it was her cousins. Each of them carried a bag that looked an awful lot like an old doctor's satchel, only these were in their signature colors.

Pink pushed past her sisters and wrapped her arms around me. "You made it, and I just knew you would!" She had tears in her brown-raspberry eyes, but she smiled through them.

"No, you didn't," said Grey as she walked into the house. "You thought she was dead. It's all you've talked about." She came over and squeezed my arm, which meant, *I'm happy to see you. I was worried.*

Gold didn't try for a hug, but she beamed at me. "We're very proud of you, Evelyn."

I had no idea what to say to any of them, so I said the first thing that came to my head: "No names!"

Gold laughed, but it wasn't a mean laugh. "Names are just fine here, now. I'm Jane. It's very nice to meet you properly."

Pink let go of me and pulled away so I could see her face. "I'm Martha, and I just knew you'd be okay."

Grey sighed, but let it go. "Evelyn, unfortunately, I'm Hyacinth."

I blinked at that. "Jane. Martha. And *Hyacinth*?" It was rude, but I said it before I could stop myself.

"Mother's idea of a joke, perhaps. But no one calls me Hyacinth." She shot her sisters a withering look as they tried to mask their smiles. "I prefer to be called . . ."

"Grey?" I asked.

The witch raised her eyebrows. "Yes, actually."

I hugged her then, because she was my favorite and because I'd known her name even when names were dangerous things.

She whispered in my ear, "I understand you gave Mother my gift?"

I nodded. "She hated it."

"Good. Thank you."

Grey untangled herself from my arms and found a seat, joining the others. Four witches sat in the four corners of the room. Each seemed tired, and they were all looking at me. They were expecting something, but all I had were questions. "How are you here?"

"Lily called, and we came," Gold—*Jane*—answered simply.

"She told us that she needed us—you needed us—so of course we came!" Pink—*Martha*—added.

"And also, we were bored," Grey finished with a smirk.

"You have a *phone*?" My head was spinning.

"It wasn't that kind of call, honey," Lily said. Right, witches.

"Thank you for coming," Lily said to her cousins. "As I explained, we have a situation and I'm hoping you can help. Since the curse happened in your neighborhood, with your rules, perhaps you'll be able to assist us in breaking it."

All three sisters nodded and spoke over one another. They would help if they could.

Lily got up and went to the kitchen. She came back with a round white platter. There were no brownies this time. Instead the platter held the collection I'd brought back from the other side of the field. And, in the center of it, the Desdemona doll. Surrounded by all that stuff, she looked even smaller than before, and the idea of fixing her seemed more and more impossible. Lily put the platter on the coffee table and the witches gathered around it. I stood back a little, not wanting to get in the way.

Martha picked Desdemona up with gentle hands and gazed at her sadly, raspberry eyes rimmed in pink. "This was just a terrible thing to do. And terribly hard to undo."

Jane touched all the items on the table, speaking softly to herself. She rummaged through her doctor's bag—I assumed it was a witch's kit—and shook her golden head.

Grey stood over the platter and crossed her arms over her chest. "None of these things will help. They're all dead things. Except the flower, of course, and it is entirely the wrong kind of curse."

Martha motioned for me to come sit next to her. When I did, she handed me Desdemona, who was still warm in my hands. "Darling, your aunt has been bound. I can't see it—my eyes, you know—but I can feel the binds around her wrists and ankles and her poor throat."

Jane spoke up, "The problem with a good binding is that it is rather like a messy knot. You need the one who tied it to untie it—"

"And he's in a cage in the field," Lily interrupted.

"And he'd never help, even if he were here," muttered Grey.

"Or," Jane continued, "you need just the right instrument or tool. Something that belonged to the person who did the binding. A tool the person would have used to do their work. Their favorite, if you will."

"Pope had lots of tools," I said to them, but I was mostly talking to Desdemona. "All sorts of things on his workbench. And I think he had a favorite, because . . ." Bird and I must have had the same idea at the same time, because he was zipping back and forth across my shoulders.

I handed Aunt Des back to Martha and half ran to the guest room. I was afraid I wouldn't find what I was looking for. Afraid they'd fallen out in my dash across the field. But in the side pouch of my backpack, my fingers closed around cold metal handles.

I brought the sewing shears back to the living room. They were old-fashioned and simple, silver metal dull from use and blades wicked sharp from years of honing. The witches adjusted their glasses to get a look at what I was holding out.

"Are those *his* scissors?" Grey asked.

"Yeah. He threw them at me. I'm pretty sure he was still trying to kill me."

"Bring them here," instructed Jane. She ran a finger over the thin blades. "These"—she looked up—"now, *these* will do."

Lily took them next. "Evelyn, when you cut the bindings, you must be very careful. If you accidentally cut Desdemona, it would be like slicing her with a poisoned razor."

Lily handed the scissors back to me.

Wait a minute.

"Wait a minute," I said. "What do you mean, when *I* cut the bindings?"

"Well, it can't be us," said Martha. "We can't see well enough. Besides, the scissors aren't ours. They're yours."

"They're not mine! They're Pope's."

"No," said Grey, "he gave them to you. They're yours."

I wasn't sure trying to kill someone with scissors was the same thing as giving the scissors as a gift. But the four witches were nodding, and Bird was giving me his little Bird nudges, and I was completely outnumbered.

All at once, the witches got busy. Martha gave Desdemona to me while Jane picked up the white platter. Grey moved the coffee table to the side of the room. Lily turned on every light she could, making the living room as bright as possible. I stood watching them work, holding Pope's scissors in one hand and my aunt in the other.

Lily stretched a coffee-colored blanket across the middle of the living room carpet. "Put her here, so there's room in case it works." She caught my eye from across the room. "*When* it works."

I rested the Desdemona doll in the center of the blanket and knelt beside her, bending low over the doll. At first I couldn't see the bindings at all. But my fingers felt them, thin strands like wound-up spiders' webs. And once I felt them, and knew where to look, I found I *could* see strands—gossamer white and finer than thread.

The four witches sat back down.
Jane looked calm—serene, even.
Martha looked like she was about to throw up.

Grey and Lily looked, well, they both looked like they believed in me.

"Um, now?" I asked.

"Whenever you're ready, darling," Martha encouraged me.

"A little help, buddy?" Bird flew into my right palm, and I checked my hands. They weren't shaking at all.

With a deep breath, I lowered the shears and snipped gently at Aunt D's right wrist. When the binding was cut, it blackened and fell away. The room felt a little different too, almost like how the pressure changes when you drive up a big hill.

The witches were silent, doing their best not to distract me.

I cut the next wrist binding, and then the one on D's right ankle. They fell away, black and burned-looking. The pressure in the room got stronger, and now it was more like being in an airplane than a car going uphill.

The witches were still silent.

With the fourth binding cut, the pressure changed again, and my ears actually popped. The Desdemona doll's arms and legs were free, but there was still the binding around her throat, and that was the one I was most worried about.

My nerves kicked into gear. This was it. If I couldn't do this one thing, this one *simple* thing, all my trying to save Des wouldn't mean anything at all. I was overthinking it and started trembling when I felt a hand on my shoulder.

I looked up and saw Lily standing over me, but her

eyes were on the front windows. Bird had moved back to my shoulder and was watching too. It was easy to see why.

Through the tiniest cracks in the window frames, a black fog was lazily seeping into the house. It twisted and churned, and I recognized it at once.

The black nothing had followed me home.

"Lily, I—"

"Shhh. Cut the last binding. Do it quick. And when you do, get away from Desdemona. Leave her there and come to me. I don't know what will happen, but I want you out of the way." Lily squeezed my shoulder quick and hard—*You can do this, brave girl*—and stepped to the kitchen doorway to wait for me. The cousins tripped over each other to get away too.

I had never imagined that anything but Pope and the shadow sparrows would—or could—follow me out of the green-black field. I was wrong about that, and wrong about being safe. I hadn't really escaped after all. The black fog would drag me by the ankles back to the other side of the gate and I'd never be home again.

I shook my head and took a very deep breath, trying to block out the nothingness and the poison blades.

I focused.

I focused on all the big and little things we do for the people we love.

I focused on all the things I'd done to save Des, things I'd never imagined I could.

I snipped the last binding.

Before the threads could finish falling away from

Desdemona's tiny throat, the swirling black poured in through the window seams and the doorframe. It found every tiny gap and crack in the house, and then the front door flew open and the nothing came rushing in like a wave. I lost sight of Desdemona as the darkness covered the middle of the floor like a spreading puddle.

"Evie!" Lily screamed for me.

"No—I have to find her!" The nothing rose like a flood. My entire bottom half had disappeared into it. The fog of darkness felt thick and clammy where it touched my skin. On my knees, I ran my hands across the floor blindly, trying to feel for the tiny doll.

She wasn't there.

I howled, and it didn't sound so different from Pope howling in the field. It was the sound you made when you'd lost the thing you wanted most.

Like a tentacle, the black nothing grabbed my hand then and it pulled, trying to drag me down into it.

"No!" I screamed. I pulled back, hard. And when I did, I realized that a pale hand with long fingers was grasping mine. Not the black nothing after all.

That hand—that regular-sized hand—belonged to Aunt D.

I dropped the scissors and pulled her hand with both of mine, trying to drag my aunt out of the growing pool in the center of the room. When her face emerged, it was bone pale, and her eyes were enormous with shock. She wasn't helping me help her. I didn't think she could.

The nothing pulled back. But it wasn't pulling at Desdemona exactly.

I had missed a bit of the gossamer binding around her neck, but it was no longer spiderweb thin. Around D's neck was a chain made of thick iron links. It was still wrapped once around her throat, one loose end hanging over her shoulder. The black nothing had the other end and was pulling it back into the churning lake of void.

I stopped trying to get Des out and rushed closer to her instead. I lashed out against the black nothing, punching and screaming as I went. I didn't know if I could hurt the fog, but that didn't stop me from trying.

Then I grabbed the short end of the chain, unwound it quicker than Mother Witch had ever moved, and freed Aunt D's neck. It was the most important thing I'd ever done, and I'd never been less anxious. I knew what to do. I was sure. The chain felt like the iron gate had—greasy and warm. I threw it as hard as I could into the churning pool.

As suddenly as the attack had started, it was over.

The black nothing retreated, slipping back the same way it had come in. Most of it disappeared through the open front door, taking with it the sound of clanking iron chains.

Des collapsed on the floor next to me. I threw my arms around her.

"Are you really here?"

She sat up slowly, gingerly touching the red, angry marks around her neck. "I'm here, baby." Her voice was a broken whisper.

"*How* are you here?" I was sobbing.

"Witches," she answered with the ghost of a smile. "And you, of course."

Arms around her, I could feel how cold she was, and that she was somehow smaller than she'd been before. Not shorter or thinner, just smaller.

I pulled away to look at her face. Her dark brown eyes had gone an overcast grey. I stared long enough to see tiny storm clouds move across her irises.

"Are you okay?"

"Okay enough."

"Are you . . . different?"

Aunt D's now-grey eyes scanned the ceiling, looking for a way to answer my question. Then, "A little. I think I left a bit behind and brought a bit back with me."

"Are you still you?" The words came out creaky because I was starting to cry again.

"Of course I am." Desdemona put a cold hand on my cheek. "I changed a little. So did you." She touched Bird, who was spinning circles on my collarbone. "But we're both still us. And we're both still here. And we're both free."

I hugged her again, hard this time, now that I was sure she was real.

While Des and I held on to one another, the three witch sisters were buzzing around the house, closing doors, grabbing blankets, and of course, making tea. Lily knelt beside us.

"Why?" I asked her. "Did it come back for the chain? Why wasn't it here for me or Des?"

"I think it wanted what belonged to it, and the dark

magic in that chain certainly felt the same. If Pope had any power at all, he borrowed it from that . . . that . . ." Lily couldn't find the right words.

"Nothing," I finished for her.

"That seems appropriate." She smiled weakly, but her eyes were on Des. "What do you need, my friend?"

Des held me close to her. "This girl, and sleep."

There would be time to tell Aunt Desdemona about my day in the strange neighborhood. And time for her to tell me her story, although I wasn't sure how much I really wanted to know. But tonight was not the time.

Des accepted all the fussing and worrying the witches proceeded to do, though not for long. Soon Lily had her dressed in a nightgown just as ridiculous as the one I was in. Then we both crawled into the guest-room bed together, my head on Desdemona's shoulder and her arm around me.

We kept the lamp on that night, and we didn't talk. Much.

"I love you, sweet girl. My brave, strong, smart Evie." She kissed me on the top of my head.

"I love you, too."

And then we were asleep.

28

Lily drove us home the next morning.

Grey's eyes got wide when she heard we'd be going in Lily's car. "It's been a very long time since I've been in an automobile. I'd love to go for a ride again."

"They're too loud. And they stink." Jane shook her golden head in disapproval. She returned to the book she was reading and did not join us.

"I think they're scary." Martha pulled her pink shawl up higher around her chin. She stayed behind as well.

So the four of us piled into Lily's beige sedan—Lily and Grey in the front, me and Des in the back. Well, five of us, counting Bird. We had one stop to make before we could go home, because we had to deal with the problem of Aunt D's car.

I was nervous. For starters, I didn't want to go back to the abattoir ever. But I also didn't want to face the police or firefighters or detectives I knew would be crawling all over the burned remains of the building.

Des and Lily and Grey promised they would handle it. That worked for me, because I wasn't so sure that telling the truth was the right way to go this time, and

I was too wrung out to think of any good lies.

Our drive across town was quiet. Lily and Grey chatted softly in the front seat, Lily pointing out what had changed since the last time Grey had been in town. Not much ever changed in Blight Harbor, so there wasn't much for them to talk about.

Desdemona and I sat, holding hands and each thinking our own thoughts. As we started down the long road that led to the abattoir, I couldn't make sense of what I was seeing.

It was still there.

Every brick and board and empty window of the abattoir was still standing. Impossible, but true. I'd watched it burn the night before—I'd burned it down myself. But somehow, overnight, it had rebuilt itself.

Other than Aunt D's car, the road and the land around the old slaughterhouse were empty. There were no detectives, because there was nothing to investigate.

"How?" I asked from the back seat. "I *told* you, I set it on fire. It was burning when I rode away." When the car stopped behind Aunt D's, the three women exchanged glances. It seemed they were each waiting for another to answer.

Finally Grey turned around in her seat to look at me. "Evelyn, I believe you. You did burn it down. You burned the parts that needed to be burned. You burned the evil out of it, the stains of all the bad things that happened there.

"But the bricks and stones and boards of the place, those aren't evil. Those are just the bones of a building.

Nothing more. The fire you set last night wasn't interested in those things."

My head swam. "Because it was lit with a magic match?"

Grey nodded, her face set and serious. "Yes. But its user was magic too. In her own way."

Witches were frustrating.

I was trying to figure out my next question when Des opened her car door and stepped into the dry grass of the abattoir yard. I got out to follow her to her car. Instead she started toward the open mouth of the slaughterhouse.

No. There was no way she was going back into that place, and I grabbed her by her arm to tell her so. She didn't give me a chance.

"I'm scared of it," she said quietly.

"Me too," I agreed. "So let's go home."

"Soon, but first I have to go back in. I have to go in and see for myself there's nothing left. Otherwise, I'll always be scared of it."

"No. You never have to go back in there ever again."

"I do, baby. Because I'm not going to live afraid. I have to go back in. And you should too."

Grey and Lily joined us in the shadow of the slaughterhouse. Lily put her arm around me. "You did it, honey. You made it safe. If you're ever going to really believe you're brave and powerful, now is the time to prove it to yourself. Not to us. To you."

Grey agreed. "I know what that match was capable of in the right hands. And yours were right. So I know there's nothing left to be afraid of. It's up to you, Evelyn, if you want to make sure you know it too."

"I won't make you," said Aunt Des as she started through the door, "but I hope you will."

"What do you think?" I whispered to my little buddy. Bird beat his wings twice. *It's up to you. It doesn't count if you don't decide for yourself.*

Witches—and aunts and birds—were frustrating. And good at peer pressure.

I squinted up into the empty eyes of the building. Except they didn't look like eyes anymore. They were just windows with the glass long gone. And the abattoir no longer felt defiant, or ready—it just felt like an old building.

Desdemona moved deeper into the slaughterhouse, and I hurried to catch up with her. It still stank, but even that smell was an old and tired echo of its former self. There were still shadows, but not thick and endless like before.

In the middle of the building, I stopped and got quiet. I listened and watched the commotion in the rafters. Birds were flitting and landing, talking to one another, perfectly content to be there.

Something else had changed. The stun shaft, an open steel tunnel just the night before, was closed. It looked as though it had melted. The roof now sagged to the floor, sealing it off. Nothing would be getting through the stun shaft again, coming or going.

Desdemona stood at the back wall. It was the same place I'd found her the first time. Even before I got to her, I could see what she was looking at—or not looking at.

All the bird silhouettes were gone. It was then I realized that I'd lost track of the little flock the night before as I made my way to Lily's house.

"Where do you think they went?" I asked.

"Somewhere they are needed, I suppose," answered Des. "If there's nothing left here to fend off or protect, their work is done."

It was enough for me. I was convinced, and no longer afraid.

Des read my mind. "You good?"

"Yeah, I actually am. Can we go home now?"

"I thought you'd never ask." Des's eyes were happy, teasing, even if they were grey now instead of brown. I hugged her hard, because that was the moment I was absolutely, totally sure she was really back.

On the way to Des's car, I grabbed my helmet out of the grass and threw it into the back seat, hoping my aunt wouldn't notice.

Lily and Grey followed us home. Lily said it was because my bike was in her trunk, but I think she really just wanted to make sure we got there okay. When we pulled into our driveway, Lily and Grey parked behind us and got out to say goodbye.

"Take tomorrow off, but I want you back at the library for your next shift and some new lessons." Lily squeezed my hand—*Nice work, I'm proud, I love you*—and went back to her car.

Grey stood with her hands on her hips, staring hard at me. Then she grabbed the tops of my arms in her hands, just like her mother had. But unlike Mother Witch, Grey's clutch was reassuring instead of painful. "I'll miss you, twit."

"I'll miss you, too. Will you come back?"

"Perhaps, but we have to get home. Martha has adopted a pet, of all things, so now we have a little fawn who'll be looking for us. He's a needy creature."

I smiled big. "I know him. Tell him I said hi?"

Grey cocked her eyebrow at me but nodded. "Remember that story for the next time we meet?" That sounded like a promise to me. I'd see her again. I hugged Grey then, and she hugged me back.

Des and I waved as they drove off. We went to the porch together and sat on the steps to take off our shoes before going into the house. Movement above me made me look up.

Scattered across the ceiling of our covered porch were dozens of familiar forms. All the little shadow sparrows were there. They hadn't disappeared from the abattoir. They had moved.

Bird danced across my back, happy to see his friends.

"Buddy, do you want to go with them?" I'd gotten used to him and wanted him to stay, but I also wanted it to be his choice.

Bird crawled up to his favorite place between my neck and my shoulder. He nuzzled me a little, then tucked his wings and settled in.

I was glad.

"Come on," Des said, taking my hand and pulling me to my feet. "I'm going to make us some tea."

This time, I didn't complain.

29

My bedroom floor was covered in a black blanket I'd borrowed from Des.

All my tools were lined up neatly. Tweezers, tiny pliers, a magnifying glass, and a tube of superglue. I'd stretched an extension cord across the room and plugged in the brightest lamp I could find in the house. I set it down on the blanket too.

The doll was on her back, faceup and staring through penny eyes. She was my last one, the last doll I had to put back together.

Eleven other dolls—and nearly as many days—had come before her. I'd taken my time with them all. Matching the right fingers to the right hands was hard, but the toes were even harder. Some of the fingers had painted nails, and that helped. But the toes were all so tiny and, well, toe-like, they were nearly impossible to sort. Putting them back on the dolls was delicate surgery.

I'd been frustrated at first. Had given up more than once.

But the penny-eyed ghosts were patient. Each sat cross-legged on the other side of the blanket as I worked on their doll. One doll at a time, one ghost at a time. They watched as I put all their little fingers and toes back where they belonged.

The first doll I finished belonged to the petite woman in the big hat. With her last toe reattached, I heard a soft thud. The pennies had fallen out of the ghost's hazel eyes and lay on the black blanket. She stood, bent over, kissed me on the forehead, and went out my bedroom door.

I was shocked, but not so shocked that I didn't follow close behind her. She went down the stairs and across our living room, and stopped at the front door. Not knowing what else to do, I opened it for her. She nodded at me as she went through. I watched as she strolled down the street, no shuffling now, and disappeared around the corner a block away.

After that, I knew what to expect, and one by one, I fixed the dolls. Each time, as I finished, the pennies fell from their eyes. They each said thank you in their own way. A kiss or a nod or a huge, happy smile.

The seventh ghost, a woman with a glamorous red dress and lipstick to match, reached up and touched Bird before she left. He puffed up proudly on my arm.

The eleventh doll was the tall man in the hat. The man The Clackity had taken over. But he didn't leave. He went down the stairs and took a seat on the uncomfortable chair by the front door. No one ever sat there, and Des said he was welcome to stay as long as he wanted.

I knew what—who—he was waiting for.

My pretty guide was the last doll I fixed. I'd saved her

until I was really good at it. I wanted to make sure I got her just right.

Her last pale toe in place, I heard the familiar *thunk* of pennies on the floor. I looked up and met eyes just as green as mine. She wriggled her fingers and scrunched up her toes. Her smile was worth everything I'd gone through in the neighborhood behind the abattoir.

My pretty guide hopped up and did a little twirl. She put both her hands on my face and kissed my cheeks. Then my forehead. Then my cheeks again. She squeezed my hands in hers—as much as a ghost can squeeze, anyway—and pressed her forehead against mine.

She didn't walk down the stairs; she glided. My friend was finally every bit as graceful as she looked.

When we got to the living room, the tall man was standing with his hat in his hand. He reached out with his free hand and my pretty guide took it, then fell into his arms. They stood that way for a minute and I looked away, wanting to give them some privacy.

When I risked looking back, they were standing at the front door. I opened it for them. The tall man tipped his hat to me as he left. My pretty guide gave me one more kiss for good measure.

Then they were on the lawn, moonlight streaming through their edges so they were illuminated with it. The tall man walked straight and proud. He tried to take my guide's hand again but missed.

She was spinning, dancing.

I stared after them long after they disappeared.

When I finally went back into the house and closed

the door, Des was watching from her chair with a sad sort of smile. "Well," she said, "that was the last of them?"

I nodded. It was bittersweet to think it was over. To know I wouldn't see any of them again. But I was happy, too. And proud. And, suddenly, restless.

It was still only June, after all, and days and days of summer blue skies were waiting for me.

I threw myself down on the couch. "Okay, then. What's next?"

ACKNOWLEDGMENTS

Every story has a beginning, and *The Clackity* would not be a book today if my sister, Georgia Oswald, hadn't sent me a random text message in October of 2018. That message, which read, "Haunts from Heloise," left me gleefully pondering the notion of an otherworldly advice column. From there, Aunt Desdemona was born, and Evie soon followed. Thank you, Georgia. This book exists because of you.

A book needs a setting, and the best settings are also characters in their own right. My hope is that Blight Harbor is one of those places. The town, and the all-important abattoir, wouldn't be here today if in July of 2019, my husband, Pete Senf, hadn't taken me to a rather cool (and most certainly haunted) abandoned slaughterhouse in his hometown of Butte, Montana. He also let me hold up our road trip while I explored and took pictures and fell in love with that old place. By the way, I met Bird there too. Thank you, Pete, for helping me lay the foundation for the seventh most haunted town in America (per capita).

To my brilliant editor, Julia McCarthy—thank you from my whole entire heart. You understood Evie from the day you met her, and love her just as much as I do. Plus, you cry at all the right parts. And you celebrate Spooky Season better than anyone I've ever met. You have my gratitude always.

To my amazing agent, Ali Herring—you took a chance on a brand-new writer who brought to you a truly weird manuscript. Then you were patient when I said, "Wait! Just kidding—that's not the story I really want to tell. *This* is the story." I sent you an early draft of *The Clackity*, you read it in a weekend, and before I knew it, we were both committed to seeing Evie's story become a real book. Thank you, my friend, for helping me figure out how to write from my heart and not just my head.

To the most talented human I know, Alfredo Cáceres— your incredible illustrations and cover art brought Evie and Blight Harbor to life. You somehow took the weird things that live in my brain and gave them bones and hearts, and faces for everyone to see. I don't know if you're some kind of magician, or just impossibly good at what you do, but I appreciate you so very much and am forever honored to have worked with you and to now call you a friend.

To the wonderful team at Atheneum/Simon & Schuster—there are so many publishing professionals involved in turning a story into a book. *The Clackity* wouldn't be on bookshelves today if it weren't for Jeannie Ng, Tatyana Rosalia, Valerie Shea, Karyn Lee, Nicole Valdez, Reka Simonsen, and Justin Chanda. Thank you all for lending your support and your time—and your gifts—to *The Clackity*.

To Sarah Jane Abbott—you know what you did, and what you did was the best kind of magic. I am grateful with my whole, entire heart.

To my small but fierce writing group—Jessica Conoley, Paula Gleeson, and Kellie McQueen—you three have been with me through all the false starts and real starts and self-doubts and celebrations. You've given me honest feedback when I needed it and encouragement when I *really* needed it. Most of all you've given me Fortitude, and I adore you for those and so many other reasons. Someday we'll all be on the same continent together.

To my early readers and constant cheer squad—you know who you are, but I want the rest of the world to know as well: Darlene Shinskie, Georgia Oswald, Anna Gamble, Bonnie Glantz, Stacy Shearer, Ruthie Dearing, and Judy Senf. Your support has meant more to me than I can express.

To my parents, Tom and Darlene Shinskie—you believed I could do this more than you probably should have. Turns out you were right (again). Thank you for that and so much more.

Finally, to my children, Miriam and Martin—it is because of you that I was able to write Evie. She is beautiful, strong, smart, and kind. I knew how to make her that way because I know *you* and am lucky enough to be your mom. I love you people more than you can possibly understand.